THE GATE OF AIR

THE GATE OF AIR

JAMES BUCHAN

LARGE PRINT
Oxford

First published in Great Britain 2008
by
MacLehose Press
an imprint of Quercus

Published in Large Print 2009 by ISIS Publishing Ltd.,
7 Centremead, Osney Mead, Oxford OX2 0ES
by arrangement with
Quercus

British Library Cataloguing in Publication Data
Buchan, James.
   The gate of air
   1. Country life - - Fiction.
   2. Apparitions - - Fiction.
   3. Psychological fiction.
   4. Large type books.
   I. Title
   823.9'14–dc22

         ISBN 978–0–7531–8388–5 (hb)
         ISBN 978–0–7531–8389–2 (pb)

   Printed and bound in Great Britain by
   T. J. International Ltd., Padstow, Cornwall

For Nick

"They say there were three of them, and their dog made it four."

Koran 18:22

CHAPTER ONE

Paradise Farm

One morning in April towards the end of the twentieth century, a woman and a man both in the prime of life drove down the lane that runs through the village of Haze Common in Brackshire, passed the stone gates of Mount Royal House and turned into the country. Harriet Woodman, an estate agent, was driving. Jim Smith, as he called himself, was the passenger. They were looking for a house for Jim to buy.

They had been too long in each other's company. A parade of comfortless buildings had wearied them. In her mind's eye Harriet saw an inferno of gravel, mouldy Jacobean stair posts, moss-infested lawns and *Cypressocyparis leylandii*. She had tried flirting, but there was something cold about the man that unsettled her and she did not like. He was neither married nor divorced, so why on earth did he want a country house? Alert since her girlhood to the shading of social character even in Londoners, Harriet found Jim Smith hard to place.

The lane, wide enough for just a single automobile, passed a farmyard and a clutter of rollers and baling machines. It turned right and left to please fields of black plough and oblong oak woods of no plain purpose. Harriet slowed down. A turn of the steering wheel, and a red brick house flickered into view, with a range of four sash windows under pointed gables, and a thicket of octagonal chimney stacks. The effect was neither sinister nor whimsical, but of some virtuous quality that Harriet could neither name nor admire. In truth, Paradise Farm was a house of ordinary appearance, square and light and feminine in the eighteenth-century British fashion, with here and there the surly remains of a much older house, which was everything but those things. Old-fashioned and inconvenient, Paradise Farm opened vistas of romantic domesticity and, once that was all done, expense without limit.

The man was looking the way they had come.

Harriet did not like Paradise Farm. It was easy to sell and if nobody stayed longer than a couple of years, well, all the better for the trade. The character of the house, not so much shopworn as restless (as a feverish child is restless), which she felt more strongly at each visit, must in the end become evident to buyers. She had an inspiration. "The perfect small country house," she said.

The man said nothing.

Harriet thought: For half of 1 per cent of the purchase price, I suppose I'd better show you the brute.

Harriet was new to the property trade. She had set up as a buyer's agent just the year before in the belief that she had an asset in her friends who had married rich men. It was a model business plan. Harriet knew every rectory, manor and hall in the county, and how each sat, as it were, in the female lap. Where others saw gardens and porticoes, and vehicles aslant on yellow gravel, woods cluttered with pheasants, lawns, swimming pools and the many badges of British rural opulence, Harriet saw women's hearts at the point of breaking. She knew who was unhappy, who was unfaithful, who was sick, broke, or mad, who was on pills or the bottle, who was on the point of flight. For such premonitions of change, the London buyers paid. For the first time in her life, Harriet had money, which she hid from her husband, her sons, Her Majesty's Revenue and Customs, and herself.

"It's not coming on the market till June at the earliest. I do have a key. But we'll have to tiptoe or Marina will murder me."

The famous name lay where Harriet had let it fall.

She parked her vehicle, and they stood before the front door while Harriet made her speech. "Paradise Farm was the dower house for Mount Royal. It's an old house that was remodelled during the Napoleonic Wars. It's just as it appears, no more, no less. No encumbrances, no subsidence, no dry rot, not liable to flooding, no pig farm, no sitting tenant, no right of way, not tight on its land, no travellers' encampment . . ." Harriet noted the man was not listening. "It's Listed Grade I, but only the exterior, so you can do what you like with the inside." She wondered why she bothered. Doesn't talk, doesn't listen. "There is one drawback . . ."

Harriet had learned in a hard childhood to conceal a large fault with a small.

"Only one?"

He speaks!

Harriet stuck to her schedule. She said: "The drawback is that there's just one way in, by that silly road we took. It's quite isolated. You can go a whole day with nothing coming by. I think that's why Marina never . . ."

She stopped. Marina never what? Never got to the shops? Never drew a sober breath? Never smiled again?

The man looked down the lane where it passed on between hedge oaks and black fields under a veil of green from autumn-sown wheat. He asked: "Where does the road lead?"

Yakkity-yakkity-yak! The chap simply would not stop talking!

"To the church, which nobody goes to any more, and the ford and then just poor Jack Bolingbroke."

The man looked up. "Why poor Mr Bolingbroke?"

"Lord Bolingbroke," said Harriet. She examined Jim. She was not sure how far he understood the social values of the district, which were anyway in commotion. "Well, he's sold Mount Royal and all the farms, has just the second house, which is small and falling down, and the park's down to sugar beets, and he's losing his sight, and he's out of the Lords. Gay, of course," she said with an open mind. Then, fearing that she had been mistaken in Jim, and that an aristocratic, bankrupt, blind and homosexual neighbour might constitute a "feature" of Paradise Farm, Harriet added: "Sweet in his way."

4

At Wanstock Manor and Branwell Hall, Harriet had seen in the first room that her client was not interested, and with good reason, but he marched on, eyes to the floor. Paradise Farm was empty of furniture and pictures, but a woman would have seen the care and expense that Marina Lampard had poured like honey on the kitchen and bathrooms and garden, as if she had wanted to live in the house herself. Maybe a gay man as well. At least, he would not want to see the outbuildings. Harriet could never remember which was the brew-house and which the forge and which the laundry and the one with the marble counters, whatever that had been for. Since the man had no children, she need not talk about the schools in the district, which were bad to the point of insurrection. Harriet preferred, all other things being equal, to speak the truth.

Had Harriet only known it, Jim Smith did take in impressions of Paradise Farm. It was as if he were pointing out to Harriet, and not she to him, the grey lichen on the red brick, and the light tumbling like new bedlinen from the sashes, and the fantastical knurled chimney stacks, and the Latin scudding over the lintel of the back door: "*Condidit has aedes Franciscus nomine Boling / Annum si domini queris . . .*" It was as though a ram were battering his barricaded Londoner's heart.

Harriet did not like to go within doors of Paradise Farm. At the best of times, it had an atmosphere like no other of her properties. Now, beneath the dust and the new paint, there was a scent she found demoralising. It was not damp, nor drains, as at Wanstock, nor dogshit, nor, as at Branwell, a dead rat in the wainscotting. The scent was costly and feminine, as if an old-fashioned wedding or dance were about to commence or had just come to an end. As the man strode towards the drawing-room, Harriet stopped dead. The man pulled open the double doors.

It was a big room, with nothing in it but a large and old-fashioned chimney piece, with more Latin cut into the mantel. Bare oak boards showed by an uneven fading where carpets had once lain. Across from the fireplace, a French door banged open and shut. One of its panes had shattered, and shivers of glass broke the sky into blue pieces on the boards. The very air seemed recomposed, as if something had passed through it, not much of anything or many of it, but lately, and taking in its train the innocence and good name of the house. Some barrier, between the outside and the inside or even between what was and what is, had disintegrated in a fall of glass and light. There was nothing else but that scent of women and greenhouse flowers, and the door banging open and shut. Jim walked across and closed it. The handle was cold to the touch. When he turned, he saw Harriet was not there.

Outside in the sunshine, Harriet had locked herself in her vehicle. She was gabbling into her telephone. Through the windscreen, she was as white as a snowdrop. Beyond her, seated on its haunches in the midst of the lawn, was a vixen. Her red hair bristled on her mask and down her back and made a ridge of her tail. Hot urine reeked between her legs. The animal

6

rose, and without taking her eyes off Jim, trotted towards the pasture. Harriet held the mobile fit to break it. Jim rapped on the side window.

"Sorry," she said, opening the electric window. "Call from the office."

"I understood you were acting exclusively for me, Harriet. Who else have you shown this house to, Harriet?"

"I just don't get it," said Harriet. "I think Marina has some chap who looks in every day. He must have left something open."

"Must have done."

You still have a chance. H. didn't get out of his pigging car. The Darks have to finance. I wouldn't live at Paradise Farm if you paid me! I wouldn't live here if you gave me all Marina's money!

Jim turned and saw grass between the cobbles in the farmyard and wall buttresses sunk deep in manure. The shaft of a dog cart stood aslant the blue sky. Gusts of vertigo blew through him. He cast up all that he had seen: a bead of oil on the teeth of a hanging spring-trap, that splash of milk on the marble counter in the dairy, the butt of a roll-up cigarette aslant where it had fallen, not an hour ago, on a wet dock leaf. He said: "You can offer the sellers what they want."

"Don't you . . . ?"

"No. Please make an unconditional offer at the asking price."

"Phew! You don't let the grass grow."

The man showed no reaction to the compliment. What a shit! What a nancy-looking, cold, stuck-up, common, nouveau-riche, queer, chippy, left-wing London shit!

"I'll call Marina this afternoon," said Harriet. She was all business. Then she touched his sleeve. "You won't mention it, will you?"

"Won't mention what?"

"About there."

"About what?"

She shivered. "Must have been poor . . ."

The businesswoman gained the upper hand. For some buyers, as is well known, a little mystery brings distinction to a house. Another would rather have a pig farm beneath her pillow or a gypsy camp on her quilt.

"Poor who, Harriet?"

"Poor Jack Bolingbroke." She looked round. "They say from here you can see six church towers."

Jim turned through three quarters of a circle and saw the thunderstruck towers of Tregawn, Witchbourne, Bablock, Misselden, Haze and St Roche becalmed amid the black plough or poking through leafless woods. The past lay before him, wintry and impenetrable. The matter, he thought, was to break through the veil that resisted his most passionate approaches and responded to his devotion with strangeness or an echo. The matter, he thought, was to step without flinching into the past, as once he had stepped into the future.

CHAPTER
TWO

John Walker

Jim Smith paid cash for Paradise Farm. Lawyers in the City of London sprang on the transaction, bound it with pink cords, taunted and tortured it for nights on end and then released it less their fees. Buyer and seller did not meet. The *Brightwell Advertiser*, in its weekly survey of the county's market for dwelling houses, saw in Jim's capricious transaction overdue signs of revival.

Jim came to his new house ahead of his things. He slept on the floor downstairs under a car blanket. Since he was not in the habit of sitting down, he did not miss furniture. He did miss London. He missed the thunder of double-decker buses and the orange street-light in his bedroom, dusty window panes, footfalls on lino, the reek of close-quarters living from his neighbour's flat in the basement, the howl of the fire engines from the station across the road. He missed the profuse gardens of the rich and those bright days in June, when all of a sudden the streets and underground trains are overrun with pretty women, all bare arms and shoulders, and the men of London somehow become invisible. He missed the scuffed and thirsty public parks of August and the masked Arab women herding their children through the dust. He missed November evenings, with the lights coming on at dusk in wet yellow streets, and the slow barges on the brimming river and the translucent purple jars, late at night, in a chemist's window by Victoria Station. He missed turning off the computers on Christmas Eve in the building in Farringdon Street, long after the last of his people had gone, and thinking, conceited man that he was: For a while, I put food and drink on a couple of hundred tables.

By day, Jim walked through rank tussocks of wet grass, torrents of wind and whipping saplings, or crept through dank lanes in his hired car. At sundown, he was blown home on gales fit to lift Paradise Farm from its moorings. He had forgotten there was such a thing as weather. Unused to the country, he drove six miles every evening to the supermarket at Brightwell to buy his dinner and a bottle of beer. At night, he would walk out and listen to the cars beating down the dual carriageway under the shaking moon. He had not known that England could be so dark at night. But for the sodium blink of the Brightwell roundabout, there was no light to dim the constellations wheeling about his chimney-pots. When Jim's furniture arrived, the gang foreman said over his tea: "Takes all sorts." For a week, Jim unpacked his things and nobody called or passed.

At noon one day, standing in the valley made by his roof, dizzy with the wide and, as it were, unauthorised, view of fields and hills, the crazy brick chimneys, the abandoned satellite dish, the flash of the sea in the air above Brightwell, Jim understood that he had never been so idle. He had worked for his living since the age of thirteen. The bustle of London and his business life had concealed a certain vacancy of mind. Jim did not read, except computer trade journals and the *Financial Times*, and had not the patience for music or television. He felt his neglected nature uncoiling like a snake in the spring sun. There would be time enough, he thought, to go over what had happened in the City, but not yet, not for a good while yet.

Jim took to sleeping in different rooms, listening to the sounds of an old house returning to habitation. Floorboards creaked as if under footsteps. Heating pipes grumbled like schoolchildren. In the rooms were the fragmentary or vestigial fixtures of a luxury Jim did not fully comprehend. There were brackets above the sashes for curtain rails and attachments for wall-lamps or *torchères*. Cupboards gaped like caves for clothes he did not possess. What a deal of do there is here, Jim said to himself, when I can lie as comfortably in straw. He thought, in a sort of euphoria, that it would take him the remainder of his life to expand into Paradise Farm. On the doors of the upstairs rooms, which looked south over a new garden of hedges and cypress trees, there were black-letter Latin inscriptions over the lintels. He tried to light a fire in the drawing-room and was engulfed in smoke. On the mantel was a motto that he could no more read than the others, only he could see it was a palindrome: *"IN GIRUM IMUS NOCTE ET CONSUMIMUR IGNI."*

One night he felt something brush his face, and the touch of lips on his cheek, and a woman's bare breast catch and slip across his chest. He woke bolt upright on the boards. It was as if a woman had descended from her own realm of knowledge and sensation. He blundered downstairs in the darkness, hoping to find who knows what, a shoe aslant against a chair leg, or a skein of stocking, or a wisp of scent amid the dust. Jim stood in the darkness, palpitating with shock, pleading with the bare boards, the boxes of reports, the dark business suits hanging on rails, the glimmer through the old windowpanes. He felt himself transformed into pure masculinity, hard muscle from head to bare feet on the boards. He knew then, as he had not known in the bustle of London, that he was only half alive and had been all those years, and would be until he found this woman who was not lost, for else how could he have seen and touched her in his dream? She had passed out into the house, along the boards or round the passage-corner to a window that showed a faint false dawn. On his knees, he searched for the gleam of a footprint. He opened the window to its lock and felt the wind over his bare chest. He felt injured by femininity. He wished he were in London, where a girl in a minicab would set him bang to rights. He wished he had never come to Paradise Farm. He wished he were asleep again that the woman might return to him and he would feel her marble breast against his and put his hands on her deep-girdled waist.

Jim must have slept, if only for a minute, for he woke in a state of body and mind that was quite unfamiliar.

Jim had absorbed the prejudice that dreams were suppressed wishes and fears that were open to interpretation. The woman who had come to him, as if from an existence parallel or coincident to his own, was none other than the incarnation of his solitude. In his business life, he had had no more time for sex than for philately or the foreign relations of Norway or the tournaments of the All England Tennis Club. Now, as he unwound like a broken spring, solitary, humiliated, idle, a stranger, all manner of wants and appetites were racing across open ground towards him. Well, Jim thought, let them come.

One morning in Jim's third week at Paradise Farm, when the sun shone and he had not slept or washed or shaved, and was wearing an overall over his shorts, a van drew up by the back door. It was a Toyota pickup. Bristling over a home-made backboard was the handle of a lawnmower, a white plastic tub of some chemical or mineral-lick and the barrels of a twelve-bore shotgun. The driver was bent, thin and dirty, like an old playing-card. He smelled of grass cuttings and fag ash.

He said: "I did the heavy work for Marina."

Jim said nothing.

"I know my way about."

"I know you do. But the property is mine now."

"I was farm manager up at Mount Royal, that is till my accident." He screwed up his face to look at Jim. "He's an honest good kind of man whatever you heard, Jack Bolingbroke." He looked away. "Not that I'm that way inclined, mind."

The notion that Lord Bolingbroke's farm manager must also be gay caused Jim to smile. He said: "Where have you put the cow?"

"The new people on the Common, they won't have grazed animals. They say the animals come into their gardens. They say the children are frightened of them." He looked up. "The children are frightened of cows."

Jim had already made up his mind. "Quite right, too. Alarming beasts. You can keep her here if you want. And the calf. Don't smoke in the byre."

"Kicks."

"I shan't be milking her."

"That's a lot of grass you have."

Jim felt as if he were being drawn further and further from his own front door. "You can get me some sheep."

"Boynton at West Bablock has some in-lamb ewes. Suffolk crosses."

"How many?"

"Many as you want."

"All right, let's stock ten acres at, say, two or three an acre." Jim was out of his depth. He retreated to firmer footing. "Don't overpay if you can avoid it."

The man bristled. "You pays for quality."

"So I've always heard. Oh, and what's-your-name . . ."

"John."

". . . John." Jim pointed at the pickup. "Don't bring uncovered weapons onto my property again."

"I'll stick it in my armpit like His Lordship, shall I?"

"What I do on my own ground is my business, John."

John swivelled. Jim Smith imagined that for John in all dealings with Londoners, armed or unarmed, the local man must prevail. Jim, in contrast, saw that his essay in the patrimonial style had broken down on its first outing, and he abandoned it without regret. Looking over John's shoulder, he saw his new fields, but not as they had up to that instant appeared to him. The different greens of the oaks, the hawthorn hedge and the young wheat, all tinged with the blue of the warm atmosphere between, receded into infinity. For Jim, who had seen nothing all his life but walls and pavements and balconies, the stanchions of motorway bridges, street lights, school playgrounds, gasometers and strung telephone lines, oil refineries, abandoned explosives factories, chimneys and advertising hoardings, an entire world simultaneously being built and destroyed, this was altogether new. Jim knew that such a landscape was a creation of accident and rural economy, yet it appeared to stand outside time, to be God-given and perfect. It seemed to him that some quality of the landscape, for which he did not have a word or definition, was being pressed on him whether he liked it or not. His eyes drank in the view like water.

John turned round and followed Jim's gaze. Jim thought he must have been a good worker, before whatever it was had gotten to him.

"What am I watching for? I bet it's those Binladens. Isn't it? You was in those regions, I heard."

"Watch for what you like. It never harms. As you see, I don't like people on my ground. If I'd wanted people

15

I'd have stayed in London. They can use the public footpath. Anybody you see, I want you to tell me."

"There's only the farmer."

"Who's the farmer?"

John peered at him. It seemed John could not believe the man's ignorance. "McCain. He farms all the ground round here. Wants to cut that stag-head oak in the field. Says it's in the way of the machines."

Jim had the impression that John and Mr McCain were not friends.

"Is that all?"

"There's blondie."

"Blondie?"

"Lady. Tall. Walks her dog off the strap."

"What breed of dog?"

"One of them women's dogs. That hunts with the eyes. Quick. She walks after harvest. When the brown hares are in the stubble. Shy. Goes off if you come near her."

"What's in the field?"

"Winter wheat."

"Can you spray and combine it for me?"

John's eyes bulged. "Gordon McCain won't like that."

"Don't you worry about all that. We'll talk about your money later. Just don't leave your cigarette butts around."

John seemed by constitution incapable of taking an order. He was masterless. He turned and climbed back into his pickup. If he was pleased at his transformation, from local has-been to the Londoner's man, he did not show it. What he had shown to Jim was that he came with Paradise Farm, and there was nothing Jim could do about it.

That evening, when the darkness had taken away all colour and a bright planet risen above the ruffled wheat, Jim saw a cow shamble down the lane. A little later a calf scampered by, and then John, swinging his bad leg. Jim thought to hear the beer sloshing in John's belly and for a while, he felt encouraged.

Three mornings each week, Jim had the company of Rose Pledger. He put an advertisement in the window of Haze Post Office and she came up in a van, a man loitering behind the wheel throughout the interview. She had worked at the Hall in the days of old Lady Bolingbroke and didn't need the money, oh no, but she liked to keep busy.

She said: "I'm not doing with John Walker, whatever you say."

Jim said: "I shan't make you, Rose."

Jim decided that whatever Rose had to say about John would come out sure enough. It did not. She worked well and left stoical messages in writing as fine as copperplate: Today we ran out of bread flour. It might have been Capt. Scott's logbook, as he stared through swollen eyelids into the desert of snow. Rose gave the impression that her information and her judgements, while derived from television and women's magazines, arose in the conversation of a select circle that met often. She liked to cook Jim puddings from the Christmas books of television chefs. Towards the end of the day, Jim would come on her granddaughter, doing homework at the kitchen table like some scholar-gypsy.

Rose was as good as her word. She would not put her hand to anything that John Walker had touched. If there were a hare on the kitchen slate in the morning, or a brace of pigeons, they were still there after she had gone, decomposing in the warm kitchen air, and Jim had to clean them with his Londoner's hands.

"How you can live here," Rose said from the sink. "In the village, there was people to watch go by."

One morning, passing the byre, Jim heard a peal of grunts and squeaks like Sunday bells in the Brightwell rows. Peering over the half-door, he saw a great black sow on her side and eight piglets arrayed at her teats. He went back to the house and brought down the kitchen scraps and stood with the sow till she had eaten. The next morning, which was fine, Jim saw John Walker in a white veil, unloading from his pickup three hives of honeybees.

CHAPTER
THREE

Windowpane

"Lord Bolingbroke?"

A tall man turned on the marble pavement. Though indoors, he had on sunglasses. His hair was long to the shoulders and flecked with white. Outside in the stable yard 'Spring Fair at the Bothy' was in full swing.

"Who wants him?"

For a nobleman in his own entrance hall, Lord Bolingbroke seemed to have limitless time for strangers. One of the circulating women made as if to steer him by the arm towards Jim.

"Lord Bolingbroke, I'm your new neighbour. Jim Smith."

"At Paradise Farm?"

"Yes, sir."

"Welcome to the Brack Country."

Nobody else had said that to Jim. Encouraged, he said: "I wanted to ask you about the picture in the hall."

"Good idea. If you need to know about a picture, ask a blind man."

The women looked at Jim in outrage. Jim could see from the concentration on Lord Bolingbroke's face that he was listening for something.

"Above the doorway in the marble hall."

Bolingbroke exhaled. He turned and threaded through the women to a place near the middle of the pavement. He had the silhouette of the 1960s: tall, long-legged, long-haired, no belly, no hips, no chest. He said: "Will you describe the picture to me?"

Jim could not. He said: "A pretty woman not wearing a whole lot except a hat on her head."

Bolingbroke turned through the ruffled Tudor boys and crinolined girls to face the picture. He lifted his chin as if, above the doorway, he could see something. He said: "Painted by Mark Neal when he was not so well known."

Jim waited.

Bolingbroke turned to Jim. He said: "What Markie wanted was something that was distinctively modern: that is, slick, cheap, gimmicky, pornographic, badly drawn and painted, expendable, garish, general, mass-produced, deceitful, irreligious, insincere, poorly made. And yet, thirty years later, it is what most interests you in my house." He smiled. "And not just you."

That was courteous, or even flattering, but went over Jim's head. Jim said: "And the sitter? Or rather lier?"

Bolingbroke was listening again as if Jim's question were of a novel or unexpected character. "Did you say Paradise Farm?"

"Yes, sir."

Through the door behind him, Jim could hear the thump of the disco.

"Well, she used to live in your house. Years and years ago. When I could see, I used to like looking at that picture."

"What was her name, if I may ask?"

"You may. Her name was Jean Thinne. She was a famous beauty of the 1960s, and at one time Mrs Lampard. I think the first Mrs Lampard."

Jim barked: "So what does the current Mrs Lampard say when she comes to dinner at the Bothy?"

"Marina? Well, they haven't come for a while. Perhaps for the reason that you were kind enough to mention."

"I didn't intend to be impertinent." Jim had wanted to interest, not to insult, Lord Bolingbroke. He felt all fingers and thumbs in this country society.

Lord Bolingbroke turned his sad face on Jim. "Would you like a drink?"

"At three o'clock on a spring afternoon, I would, please."

Bolingbroke opened a door and ushered Jim out of the world.

Wide and worn wooden stairs ran down into cool darkness. A little light came in from grilles at floor level, and also voices, and the whirr of the disco. As his eyes became used to the gloom, Jim saw that the white walls were lined with wine bins. Lord Bolingbroke was listening, to Jim and to the disco.

"Choose anything you like. There should be a glass somewhere."

Jim put his hand into one of the bins and pulled out a bottle. The label said Château Something and 1982.

Jim had an idea that the wine might be too old, but did not wish to rummage through Lord Bolingbroke's cellar. He found a corkscrew and two glasses. He poured one for Bolingbroke and put it in his hand.

"What is it? I can't tell the difference between white and red."

Jim poured for himself.

"It's red."

The wine was cold, and black, and sweet as dates. The sort of wine, Jim thought, to put a giant or ogre to sleep. There was no chair, but he stood two wine boxes together for Bolingbroke to sit on, and himself leaned against the icy bricks.

He said: "Can you not taste if you can't see?" Jim had never talked to a blind man.

"If you tell me the wine is red, it is red," Bolingbroke said. Jim thought to hear a hint of impatience in his host in saying things that he had settled on years ago. "The world is not as I see it, because I can't see. The world is as you have told me it is."

Jim felt it better to shut up. They drank their wine and listened to the music bouncing about above them off the brick courtyard:

> Mama died and left me reckless
> Daddy died and left me wild, wild, wild . . .

Bolingbroke spoke at last: "If I had known when I was young that I would hear that song in my dog days, I would not have played it so often with my friends."

The sentence sounded like a self-conscious exercise in conditionality or, rather, in regret. Then Bolingbroke pulled himself together. He said: "Markie couldn't abide her. The whole of one summer, he stood there in the hall, hissing: 'Lie still, you bloody fish!' Not that Jeanie took any notice."

Jim could not tell if the recollection was painful to Bolingbroke or a pleasure. "That would have been 1967. We were listening to *Leaves of Fire* and reading . . ."

He paused.

". . . swinish books." He laughed and became Mark Neal again: " 'Leave your damn snatch alone! Nobody's interested.' "

Jim thought that era was vivid to Lord Bolingbroke, to a degree that the present was not. Was it merely a fact of nature, that he was young in that summer, fashionable, loved and was loved, could see, had money, was a lord when that meant something in England? A new song invaded the cool cellar and their reverie. Bolingbroke said: "Without death, life would be intolerable."

Whatever Jim had expected, it was not that. "And the other way round," he said.

Bolingbroke was silent, seemed in the face of Jim's levity about to drop that line of conversation, picked it up again. He said: "I mean that for one man, a railway line ruins the view from his door, but not for his children, who know nothing else but hate the houses crowding in, but not for their children, who are deafened by the new airfield. So history proceeds in a series of small injuries which would be insufferable in a single lifetime. And, even," he looked up in Jim's direction, "even if all the amenity of British life were extinguished, if all were noise and glare, somebody from a less fortunate or ruthless country might still find contentment here."

"I suppose if my family had been here for five hundred years, I would be in favour of death."

Bolingbroke took a rebuke that Jim had not intended. He asked: "Do you have a family?"

"No."

Bolingbroke turned his head as if he was looking at Jim through one eye. It was the remnant or phantom of some gesture when he could see.

Jim said: "Where is she now?"

"Who?"

"Blondie. In the picture."

"What brings you to Paradise Farm, Mr Smith?"

Jim saw he had gone too far. He must serve his time in the district before he would be admitted to such rural intelligence.

"It's a nice house in nice country. Not so easy to find nowadays. I was looking for a place with half an acre near the M21. I lived in London for some years, made my career in business. I wanted to try something different."

After four weeks in the country, Jim's autobiography sounded to him flat and wearisome, but that was nothing to its effect on Lord Bolingbroke, who rose to his feet.

"Please call again. I am not so well stocked with neighbours as I would like."

Jim felt for a place to put down his glass.

Bolingbroke went before him. With one foot on the step, he said: "If I were you, I would put pretty Jeanie from your mind."

Jim stepped out of the house into the windy sunshine. Walking across the stable yard, where automobiles had embedded the gravel in the clay, he saw the world in an altered light. He was not used to wine, or lords, or stumbling into an intimacy with strangers, as on a cracked street pavement, but yet he was not ready to ascribe his mood solely to those three novelties. Setting out down the overgrown ride to the ford, he resolved that, if there were any advantage to be drawn from his rural life, it was that in it he would learn to see. For the first time in his life, he would use his eyes.

In this mood, he splashed through the ford and was turning to Paradise Farm when he saw that his lane did not, as Harriet Woodman had said, end at the ford, but continued along the home bank of the brook. Viewed from the Bolingbroke side, he could go either to the right to Paradise Farm or strike left into new country. At any other time, he might have preferred to leave that direction a mystery. The path might lead to nothing more than a fly-tip of refrigerators or a clamp of sugar beets barricaded behind sprouted straw bales. He preferred his illusion. Yet Jim was ever prey to optimism. Somewhere around here, he said to himself,

I heard that it was beautiful, a little bit to this side or to that side, just the fraction of a step.

Why had he come to Paradise Farm? Jim had not been honest in his answer to Lord Bolingbroke. He had drifted westwards till he had come to the Atlantic and there was nowhere further to go. He had been engaged, he saw after his month in the country, in a flight from London and had turned about when he came to Brightwell, like a wallet-thief in a blind alley. At least, Jim said to himself, I'm only a fool and not a crook.

A church stood on its own at the end of a small wood. If there had been a village all those years ago, it had gone, strung out across the field so it couldn't be found, or succumbed to disease or disaster or Mr McCain's plough. The wind set the clouds racing past the square tower and shook the daffodils in the churchyard. In the porch, a gate of chicken wire banged on its hinges. On a board to the right, parish notices were dimpled with moisture. Flower vases stood in the corner, stained an indelible green.

The oak door to the nave was open. The interior of the church was bare, the walls lime-washed. Jim had almost no familiarity with churches, but it seemed to him, in his new frame of mind, that the bare walls were bare not because nothing had been put there, but because something had been taken away. They had been painted white so as to hide something; just as the screen on the way to the altar had been cut in a straight line at waist height to take something from view. Something was still quick about the place. The air was in a vibration, as if from running feet.

26

Where is everybody? thought Jim. Am I the only man in Brackshire?

Jim walked round the church. The grass was not mown. No doubt the authorities at this place, if there were any, were waiting till the daffodils were over. From one of the box tombs, the roof slab had been prised open by a bramble root as thick as a wrist. A greenfinch wheezed from atop a thorn-tree. Jim said to himself: The world is not as you see it is, only as you have been told it is. Describe what you see, not what you know. For the first time in your life.

With his back to the porch, Jim could see, rising through woods, another church tower. Intrigued, he walked round to the north side of the church, and saw a third tower on a hill. The three were aligned as if by a medieval theodolite. At the end of the yard, beside an old oak tree and a hedge open to the plough, Jim found a monument. It was of limestone, weathered and spattered with lichen. With his pocket knife, he cleared the lichen from the inscription:

In Your Charity Remember in Your Prayers
JEAN THINNE
Who Was Seen at This Place at 8a.m.
on 11 August, 1967
and not Again in this World Below.

So, Jim thought, that's why Maria What's-her-name never whatevered at Paradise Farm. Bad enough having her predecessor bare-arsed on the wall of the Bothy, let alone a mystery that haunts the public woods and crossroads, flitting over the cold hedge banks or these empty fields. Jim walked away, and then, because he had overlooked something, turned back. A sprig of primroses and violets lay tied with ribbon beneath Jean Lampard's monument. Jim looked again at the bouquet, determined that it must yield its meaning to the force of his concentration. It was not the kind of bouquet he might have left, or Lord Bolingbroke or John Walker or any man. It had been made with care and in misery. Those flowers had been picked at early morning by a woman or a girl. Panic took hold of Jim. Flint, silence, greenfinch, oak tree, splashing rain. He found himself striding through the graves, and turned for his sleepless house.

That night, Jim must have slept, for he woke to a room flooded with afternoon light. A woman pulled a curtain to, then another, breaking the light into a beam. The room smelled of tobacco and dried roses. Jim sat upright. He said: "*Quid est Mulier hominis confusio insaturabilis bestia continua solicitudo indesinens pugna quotidianum damnum tempestas domus castitatis impedimentum viri incontinentis naufragium adulterii vas inconcisum proelium animal pessimum pondus gravissimum aspis insanablis humanum mancipium?*"

"Are you talking to me?" The woman pulled her dress over her head. She had no other clothes on. The dress, which Jim had thought so pretty, and had made her so pretty, was, he now saw, a mere disguise that allowed her to pass in the world. (Once, in Moscow in the rain, Jim had seen a girl, in a new red coat and red shoes, run, head bowed, through the stage door of a burlesque theatre, and had a weakened version of this sensation. Indeed, Jim concluded, with the remains of his waking consciousness, that the sensation of that afternoon in Moscow was here revived but multiplied beyond computation in intensity and authority. Even as he passed back down into sleep, he resolved that all dreams could be decomposed into waking sensations, and that nothing was seen or heard or felt in sleep that had not come in through the gate of the senses.)

She stood in the afternoon light, as if the light was coming from her own body, from her breast and eyes and where her dress had been. He understood that this was happiness of a different order, and real to a degree that nothing in life would be. He saw that this was the best of life and not a day of his life would pass without thinking of it, and that it would be the last image imprinted on his eyes as they closed for ever. There was an alteration in the light, and in the way in which the furniture existed in the light. Objects that had seemed familiar were stripped of their familiarity. They suffered in the light. It was as if every surface reflected a facet of her beauty, as she bent on her knee to recover her dress. Jim ached with her nakedness. His arms and legs were as lifeless as fallen branches. He understood that love was of a power and force of a different order from anything else beneath the sky, and could demolish not merely family relations or notions of right and wrong but also what was real and what was not. Jim's world had been knocked a little out of its axis, and would not be restored.

She turned to him. Her face had taken on her nudity or rather had shed a veil it wore for the world. She said: "Perhaps you'd like to take off your shorts."

"Do I have to?"

"I think you do."

He felt that if he touched her breast she might be brought down to earth. He touched the round breast and hard bead at its tip. He felt something else fall from her, like a garment, as she leaned one knee on the bed. Light billowed out of her, and warmth in damp gusts as if from a garden after a rainstorm. She did not seem to be a woman, but something altogether stronger and sweeter. A darkness engulfed him, like a wave breaking over him in the sea shallows, and when he opened his stinging eyes he saw her pretty face before him.

"What about your husband?"

"Sod him." She seemed to have forgotten she had one.

Jim felt strong, and handsome, and armed to the teeth. He felt like a barefoot runner, a wrestler, a charioteer. He felt his childhood receding from him, and he felt not the smallest regret. No more the poor fatherless orphan for him! He was an outlaw and all the better for it!

Twenty-two womens
Out of the Hampton Hotel,
Twenty-six off of South Bell,
Twenty-nine women out of North Atlanta . . .

Jim seemed to have joined some mainstream of beauty and pleasure that flowed undiscovered through his world.

"Is that better, lad?"

Jim said: "Jeanie?"

"Yes."

"Why are you so nice to me?"

"Because I like you."

"Oh." Jim had thought her purposes were educational. He recognised that he had a lot to learn about women.

"And because I want you to do something for me."

"I'll do anything for you."

"Sssh. Not now."

"Jean?"

"Yes."

"What did Lord Bolingbroke mean?"

"Don't take any notice of those hippies. They're tripping."

Jim lost his confidence and with it the self-evidence of his dream. He was beginning to wake. He descended one more time.

"Are you tripping?"

"Of course. Now, shoo, go and do the cows. I'll come on to help with Bramble. And wash your hands! And when you're done washing them, wash them again!"

Outside, the hot gravel path and trees were transsubstantiated. They were touched with the essence of this woman. The whole bright world seemed to Jim saturated with femininity, and every turning of a hedge or patch of shade was an ambush, made to trap the unwary youth, rob him of his strength and wits and

31

heart. He saw, of a sudden, why women were so content in themselves. The world was theirs for the taking. Such was their dominion over men that, were they not so pleasure-loving or good-natured, there was nothing on earth that they could not command.

Jim wanted Jeanie with him, to reassure him that the world was not changed. A honeybee buzzed in the stifling stable. In the byre, two bony cows were tethered to iron rings at a trough, with an iron hurdle between them. Their tails had been tied to the rafters, beside blackboards saying "Bramble" and "Cherry" and some figures. As he pressed his head into Bramble's hot flank, he kept expecting to see Jeanie framed in the stable doorway. He hoped she would not say something indecent.

He turned. In the aura of light in the doorway stood Jean Lampard, dressed for milking. Jim wondered why women always looked different and always so beautiful. They had so many clothes and so many different ways of doing their hair. She had on jeans and a milking-coat of sparkling whiteness and a scarf for her yellow hair.

"Show me your hands, boy."

She held them in hers, turned them over, then unpicked Jim's wristwatch and gave it to him.

"Now, I'll show you once with Bramble. One jug of barley in the trough. Like this. Sit down." She pushed him down onto a three-legged stool. "Head into the flank. Like this. Now start one-handed. Give me your hand. Tits are pretty much the same across creation. You'll learn that soon enough."

CHAPTER
FOUR

Billy No-Mates

"You said you could milk."

"I did not, John. You said I could milk."

John looked round for somewhere for Jim to wash his hands.

"I brought down some hot water," said Jim.

Jim washed his hands in the bucket, and dried them on the straw. Then he squatted down and thumped his head, as the calf had done, into Bramble's flank. He began to pull. Nothing happening.

From the next-door byre came the complaining of the calf. Jim felt a sensation in his hands as if a trap or sluice had suddenly opened. The bucket began to tinkle and then, as it filled, to splash.

"Good girl, Bramble," he said.

To rest his aching back, Jim sat down on a three-legged stool.

"They want showing, they do."

Jim was too engrossed in his success with Bramble to heed what John was saying. Bramble shifted her weight.

"Watch out!"

Jim swung the bucket and his head out of the way. Bramble's near back leg kicked air.

"Bucket off the floor! Bucket never touches the floor!"

All right, all right.

"Dam and grandam were Show winners."

Shaking his head, John walked out of the stable. He appeared torn in his mind about something. Jim wondered if John was going to leave him. Well, he would live. He had learned in business never to try and keep a restless employee.

The milk, five litres of it and as many of Bramble's chestnut hairs, was pronounced fit only for the sow.

John said: "Do you want to see something?"

In the back of the pickup, a young dog tottered on four short legs. He was all out of proportion: big eyes, big ears, big nose and a body no bigger than a terrier.

"I mean for the security. You don't use them lights and televisions that people have."

"Remind me, John, when a yellow Labrador puppy last did something for somebody's security?"

Jim's witticism fell flat. John stared at the ground. He said: "He's a good dog."

He looked a good dog.

"How much do you want?"

John opened his hands. It seemed he didn't really want to sell.

"If he's as good as you say, I'll give you £200. What's his name?"

John looked at the puppy in pain.

"That's up to you."

"What did you call him?"

He mumbled.

"What?"

"Argos."

"Argos? Like the catalogue store on the ring-road?" John mumbled.

"What are you using to train Argos?"

"He likes a toy. And pieces of dried pig's liver if he does well."

"I'll make some. By the way, John, which is the church you see at the end of the lane to the west?"

"Winterbourne."

"No. Has a tower. It's not on the Ordnance Survey."

"That would be Haze St Mary. It's what they call redundant. Folks go to the car boot now. Or the Tab. at Brightwell."

"And why not?"

That evening, Argos and Jim walked round the kitchen table. Jim led him by a yellow rag doll that the dog had found from somewhere in the garden or fields. At each circuit, Jim told him to sit. After two hours, Jim gave up.

Jim said: "Try again tomorrow. Don't worry."

Argos lay on a piece of carpet near the stove, a yellow agglomeration of confusion and misery. Jim read and wrote and telephoned and sent his email standing in the hall with his back turned. The dog followed him out of the kitchen and stood by him and followed him back. In the end, Jim took him out to the doghouse in the barn. As he closed the gate, he said: "I'll come as soon as I wake up. Don't worry about anything."

The dog tried to push his nose through the bars. Jim said: "Argos, you must not give your life to me. I may not be here very long. You must learn to look after yourself."

Argos pushed his nose against Jim's hand.

Out of idleness, Jim kept a diary. Day six was the last day Argos pissed on the floor of the house. Day eight he was sitting to order. Day twelve he was going down on his belly to order, and without the toy to follow down. It was some time before Jim understood that his dog was not a human being, and did not look through Jim's commands to some purpose. He had no comprehension of Jim's purposes. At the end of the lane where it met the public road, Argos lay down and waited for Jim to come up. He did this because Jim had spent four and a half hours making him do so. He wished to please Jim. Jim doubted he made the mental connection between the triangle of Jim's hand gesture, the toy or the nugget of dried liver, and the laden sugar-beet lorries of J. A. McCain Haulage, pounding past and cracking the bridges as they went over. Argos wished to please Jim.

What Argos could not tolerate was Jim's displeasure. If, because he was teething or for some other reason, he chewed the edge of a carpet and Jim scolded him, he lay on his back or put his muzzle in the air, as if star-gazing, but in reality baring his belly, throat and testicles for Jim to rip with his teeth. Jim's heart would melt and he would say: Don't give your life to me. I am not worth it.

In the morning, Argos roamed the farm or sat with Jim while he worked. At noon, he would come to find Jim and show him some new toy turned up from somewhere in the field or barns, a football or a stuffed toy cat still wet from the long grass and leaves. It was as if the place had once been overrun by profligate children who survived only in what they had lost. Jim did not care to think that once there had been children at Paradise Farm.

"She liked it here," said John, smelling of beer and taking the toy from Argos.

"Who liked it here?"

"The little one did." He cast a look up to the large oak by the gate. "In clear weather, I was to go up with my gun and smokes to keep an eye."

"John, are you telling me that Mrs . . ."

"Marina . . ."

". . . asked you to guard her child while it played outside?"

John said nothing. It seemed to Jim that John had not intended to say so much. Also that though Jim might pay John's wages, he was not fit to latch the little shoe of John's timorous former employer. Jim closed the subject, he hoped for all time. "I think we should collect these things up and send them on to Mrs Lampard."

Jim walked to the oak. He had not noticed that there was a spiral staircase round the bole, and a trapdoor through a platform laid across the first fork of the tree. There was barely room for Jim to climb and haul himself up. The house was well made. The imagination of a child had been brought to life in the skill of an old-fashioned carpenter. There were rope ladders that stowed away out of sight, camouflage netting that raised on a pulley, and a sort of aerial slide to a platform on the next oak. On the plank floor were waterlogged fag ends and spent shotgun cartridges. From between the boughs, Jim could see the whole lane from Ladies Wood to the ford. At the foot of the tree, Argos was waiting, as if Jim had been up to heaven for a night and a day, and returned.

Every afternoon, Jim walked the roads with his dog. He was surprised that, in such a crowded land as England, he saw nobody. There was nobody on the lanes, or working in the fields, or in the scattered houses that he passed. If he came on someone, an old dame standing dazed before her cottage with a lame terrier under a smoking chimney, she would recoil from him as if he were a straggler from some broken army, and then scold and scold and scold.

Jim felt, as he had in the church, that it had not always been so. Where were the people he saw at the supermarket? Why weren't there lovers throwing their bicycles down among the weeds? Where were the moody young men who had stayed behind? They seemed to have passed under the fields, and the whole country, with its green barley and broad trees, existed only to please him and Argos. Only if he were out at three in the afternoon would he see the little school mothers and their children, elevated high above the fields and hedges in their vehicles, and then there was nothing till the barn owls came out to hunt the tummocks of the rough pasture and the white-van men came home to their pretty wives.

Jim had an eye for the profit in any activity, and in each lane he saw signs of an agriculture in its final phase. Here were gigantic machines that churned up the verges and cracked the bridges, thousand-acre fields, the same variety of crop repeated over and over, hills of sugar-beets on concrete aprons by the roadside, hedges along which a flail had been dragged, as if browsed by some monster with blunt teeth. So much capital and so few men, thought Jim. The land looked as if it had been whipped by agriculture, as if for some repeated misdemeanour.

What was not beaten was neglected. The hedges were gapped at the root, and had to be reinforced with stock fence. The oaks in them were choked with ivy. In the immensity of plough, water stood in the tramlines and looked as if it would never dry out. The little woods, each with its pheasant feeder, should have been thinned a quarter-century ago. Jim supposed that at some era, perhaps fifty years before, perhaps forty, the people had stopped caring about the fields and woods and lanes. Some catastrophe had come on the land which historians or archeologists of the distant future would attribute to plague or pestilence or warfare, but may have been nothing more than the tractor and the combine harvester and the dismissal into other occupations of thousands of men and women.

When he came to mend his own fences, Jim was baffled by his implements. He thought it was only by intention that the post-driver or the wire-strainer could be so lubberly. Jim was strong, but he wondered how a man less strong or a woman would unravel barbed wire

or carry a straw bale or put in a straining post. With his
habitual self-assurance, Jim thought: I could sort this
lot out in no time. Then he came to himself and
recognised that he was not the only businessman in the
country nor even the most ingenious, and that a long
wave of prosperity, going back at least to the outbreak
of the Second World War, was now receding. The land
was about to enter, or had already entered, an
endgame, in which nobody need apply much ingenuity,
but much cash was still there to be extracted. For a
patient businessman, here was opportunity, but Jim
gave no thought to the matter.

As his eye became accustomed to this monotonous
farm landscape, with nothing to disturb the sky but
church towers and the lighthouse and grain bins at
Brightwell, Jim became aware of vestiges of an
obliterated industry. In among the tedious plough,
where the elevations were as faint as the depressions
were shallow, were inexplicable sunken lanes that
plunged below the roots of coppiced sweet chestnuts or
followed their own ways like cats, or the fragments of a
hedge of ash or hawthorn, which had been cut at the
root and renewed two or three or four times, and stood
out against the wind like a tramper. Marooned at the
edge of a village or beside a plantation of larches were
little woods with quaint trees Jim had never seen
before, or by The Maiden brook, waterlogged pastures
too small or oblong to merit the drainage.

Jim was no romantic. If these places were beautiful
— and Jim thought them beautiful — it was as the
residue of a landscape in which he would have felt at

peace for he thought it was abundant and industrious and free. Out in the fields, where the wind whipped up the dirt into his eyes, a single tree showed the extension of a wood or hedge that even McCain had not been able to grub up. At every bend of The Maiden, he came on the remains of a corn mill, or a bone-crushing or bark-grinding mill, a starch-, cole-, snuff- or mustard-crushing mill, button mill, tanning mill, sewage mill, yarn-spinning mill, sawmill, pumping mill. Here and there were relics of another civilisation — park trees and obelisks and long, dilapidated walls and gates shored with barbed wire — that told of lost lives of ease and pleasure. Even in the most anonymous landscape, where the new houses tumbled like supermarket boxes onto the Brightwell ring road, with their backs to the town and their faces to the traffic, where all relations of space and time had been pulverised by the automobile, Jim saw the ghosts of hard-working men and women. He thought that at some time, long ago, Brackshire must have been the richest place in England and the most free.

Jim was picking wild oats from his wheat when he saw a Land Rover stop on the road. He continued for a while, stepping in from the tramlines left by the tractor that had sowed the crop and pulling out the oats waving just above the green wheat. A breeze ruffled the wheat and showed, here and there, the beginnings of green ear.

He was embarrassed to be witnessed in this peasant activity, but persisted out of mere obstinacy. It occurred to him that he and Argos might be causing more loss to his yield trampling wheat stalks than by leaving the oats to seed. The Land Rover stayed where it was, as if it had all the time in the world.

Jim recognised that in this strange country he had lost some confidence in his own judgement. He walked down the tramlines to the hedge on the lane, where Argos was standing, on his toes, coat a-bristle. The man in the Land Rover was speaking on his mobile.

"Can I help?" said Jim through the window. A collie dog hurled itself at the meshed back of the Land Rover. Argos whined and jumped up.

The man continued speaking on his phone. Jim despised him for his bad manners, and also himself for taking them amiss. At last, the man snapped the telephone shut.

"I was going to ask you the same thing," he said.

That was not a question. Jim had to proceed. "I'm Jim Smith. I've just moved here."

"We wondered who you were. Get down, Bobby!"

Jim noted the "we". The man looked into the field.

"So now you're roguing oats."

"May I ask who I'm talking to?"

"I'm McCain. I drilled this field."

"John Walker told me."

He ignored the name. "Marina wanted evening primroses. Or was it borage? Or was it greater-crested newts?" He shook his head, as if to say: Marina didn't have a clue, either, silly cunt. "I drilled winter wheat, ten stones an acre."

Jim found his dislike of the man growing with each moment. It seemed to Jim that for Gordon McCain, he was as negligible as Mrs Lampard. In time, the field must inevitably revert to its natural owner, who was Gordon McCain. Jim said: "I take it you got my letter."

McCain said neither yes or no. He did not look the man to read letters or to write them. Letters were beside the point, which was that the field and the crop in it were his by right. He said: "We were wondering why you came here."

Jim noted that "we" again. Was it McCain and his sons? Or was it the two-thousand acre men shadowing one another at the Royal Brightwell and West Show, or racing their Rolls-Royces on the Brightwell New Cut, or cracking with the syndicate on cold shooting mornings four days a week?

"It's a nice enough place. Will you excuse me?"

McCain would not excuse him. "I can have the oats sprayed. Ten pound an acre. Save your hands." He laughed.

Jim had turned down seven from John Walker.

"No, thank you," he said. It seemed to Jim there was something else in here, much closer to hand, and not at all important.

McCain took another look at the field. What did he see? Wheat? Wild oats? Money? He murmured, "What a pity. What a great pity."

"No doubt we'll meet again," said Jim. He whistled for Argos and then, when the dog continued with his feet on McCain's bumper, called him.

Jim raised his hand in farewell and set off down the tramline. Argos followed with reluctance. When Jim looked up, a few minutes later, the Land Rover was still there. McCain was speaking on his telephone. Jim watched till the vehicle moved away.

All pleasure and reward had gone from his work. Argos was staring at him, as if by sheer concentration to divine what was upsetting his friend's mood.

"He's right, lad," Jim said out loud. "We won't be here very long. Then he can have the field all to himself to grow whatever he likes on it." He looked down at the dog. "And you and I will go somewhere where you can run . . ." Jim was embarrassed at the sentiment. "Anyway, I'll never let you down."

As he walked back to the house and squabbling rooks, Jim's spirits rose. McCain just wanted the subsidy on the field, and was the loser in the exchange. If he had been a little courteous, he might have had both the crop and the subsidy, which maybe was not much on fifty acres, but was better than nothing. McCain had become used to bullying when he could more profitably have bargained. He seemed to Jim to be a man who could not approach a house except through a gap in the hedge, along the kitchen-garden wall, past the scullery window, in through the open back door. With such comforting illusions, Jim went into his house.

Jim's novelty outraged the county. One neighbour said he was a crook, another that he was Left, another that he was not the marrying sort. One had heard from somewhere that he was chippy. Another, who had more exact information, reported that he was a damn dull dog. Though nothing was said, it was decided by a consensus or silent agreement that if they ignored Jim, perhaps he would go away.

Jim intrigued the single mothers in the villages. Jim, who had no experience at all of women, attended disordered suppers in cottage kitchens. At these entertainments, he was kind, even affectionate to the women, unravelled puzzles in their personal computers and took an interest in their sons. Yet, in some degree, Jim did not suit. His devotion to business, and utter failure in the life of the heart, had left him without experience in the ordinary purposes of humanity and made him insupportable to others. His coldness disgusted women as his arrogance exasperated men. His very lack of allegiance, to district or political party or pastime or social class, so natural in the metropolis, struck these people as suspicious or worse. Brackshire's interest in the handsome Londoner was exhausted by dinnertime. When it got about that John Walker was working at Paradise Farm, the indifference of the villages became something altogether less hospitable. That, however, passed behind Jim's back.

Jim was waiting, though for what he did not know. He was waiting for the ewes to lamb and the bees to make their honey. He was repairing rails where Bramble smashed them like matchwood for a particular tuft of grass, and spending all day with John pruning the apple trees back to productive stock, and hosing down the sow, and clearing out and replanting the fruit-cage, and feeding the ewes so they would have some milk for their lambs. He drove to a decayed industrial estate on the other side of Brightwell and bought needles, syringes, feeding tubes, artificial colostrum, hypochlorite solution, long latex gloves and iodine spray. The shelves in the warehouse were half-empty, and Jim wondered if he was to be the final customer.

Sometimes, at the end of the day, John would sit down and smoke a hand-rolled cigarette and Jim would stand and listen to what he had to say. He liked to hear John tell the story of his life, which — for a man who had never been abroad or to London, had never married or been seen to court a woman, and was hated by the countryside — was full of interest and variety. With every task John undertook, he sought a more economical or philosophical manner of doing it.

"And why did you stop the birds?"

"Nobody would pay, would they? They'd peer at the stonechat or the pied flycatcher, and say: I'll give you three quid for the pair, though I doubt I could shift them. They thought you could breed wild songbirds just like that. So then I did the ties . . ."

Since his "accident", whatever that was, John had made jewellery till he had no more lady customers, steel ties and straps to hold lorry loads, tomato plants in polystyrene tubs (a penny a seed sold for a pound). For a year or two, he kept a cattery and made fire-irons and -baskets for the newcomers to the district. His ewes grazed churchyards and roadside verges and school fields. Everything the villages threw away John recovered and put to use. Jim admired his employee's ingenuity and his determination to stay where he was, and, if there was no work, to make his own employment. It was as if he were confined to the parish of Haze by the justices of the peace or some cruel Act of Settlements. The fields and woods were not just his livelihood, but his prison.

John's life was simultaneous, and Jim had some trouble putting a date to the chief events in it. Which was the year old Bolingbroke brought in the tractors or the year the last wherry came up The Maiden from Brightwell or the year McCain burned the mill buildings to stop the children, as he said, from playing in the machinery?

John seemed to have no parents, but to have come into the world in his overall, ready for any kind of work. His first memory was filling herring barrels with sand to keep the Germans out of Tithe Street and The Hard in Brightwell. In the very cold winter, which must have been 1947-8, John was sent out by Lady Bolingbroke to bring milk from Temple Farm and did not return till spring. Mrs Pledger was kind enough to give him the remains of the roast in the kitchen, so it must have been a Sunday, and he felt it become light in the hot room and looked up and snow was falling quiet as feathers. At bedtime, he went out with Mr Pledger with storm lamps and the dogs and a ram on a ten-foot halter, to collect all the sheep and pen them in the lanes for the snow was drifting. The sheep all survived, every single one of them, by trampling on top of the snow with their feet and breaking down the drifts to ice. Mrs Pledger told Rose to make him a bed in the kitchen and then it was up before light to milk the cows. No milk left the farm for six weeks. They churned it into butter and stacked it under road salt in the dairy. Rooks and jackdaws came to the kitchen door to be fed with the poultry. Then there were five hundred ewes to lamb, which meant five weeks night and day before John was able to sleep again in a bed. He was very thin by the time spring came.

What were the Pledgers thinking? Working a ten-year-old to the very point of death? Or was life hard for everybody that winter in Brackshire? What had John done to make Rose Pledger hate him so? For a while John worked as a runner in the Black Branch, the remains of the trade on Jackdaw Hill in Brightwell for mourning clothes for ladies, taking telegrams to the post office and finding milk for the cats, four shilling a week for twelve hours a day. Was that before or after the year of the high water, must have been 1952, when they had taken the wherry across three fields from The Maiden to the Navigation, greasing the poles, the hardest day's work he'd ever done as soon as he sits here, two men, thirty shillings, fifteen shillings each, they had food in a frail basket, if you know what that is, but they'd live on beer going down there and coming back, that was wherrymen in those days. For the hardest time of all, John reared chickens across the joists in the upstairs rooms of an abandoned house, which John did not name but Jim knew was Paradise Farm.

Where had he learned to read and write?

Mavis, Lady Bolingbroke taught him his letters from a book called *Native Breeds of Cattle in Great Britain*.

Why did he count the sheep *unna dunna wether tether pip*?

Old Frank Pledger had counted sheep that way.

What came after *pip*?

Highter skighter scarer darer dick.

Jim could see his employee asleep on a cargo of rushes in a barge, or walking some sodden dusk between pollard willows under a saturated sky, or lifting potatoes in a line of fluttering skirts, or taking his tea all alone at the end of the counter in the covered market in Brightwell, moody and long-haired and dazed. To Jim the man seemed a link, perhaps the last in the district, to a time when something was done in Brackshire. John Walker had heard mills creak, seen corn threshed and cloth woven, watched young men and women walk along flowering hedgerows, or stop to kiss in the hollow ash, or steal the ripening peas. In Jim's imagination, John had watched the Dutch come a-fishing for the herring (heavy, droll, bearded men with trousers wide as sails and great shoes of willow-wood), the ships and boats passing and repassing, the seas like cliffs and the wind whipping the waves through the carriage windows and onto the ladies' dresses. Apart from John Walker, there was nothing. All around, the farms and mills had been turned into holiday cottages, the mill races mere streaks of rotten brick in the fields, and McCain's plough levelled everything.

If Jim liked to tease John Walker, he had but to mention McCain. McCain was all that John most hated in agriculture, a man for whom a timber tree was an abomination, but no more to be resisted and defeated than a crooked fence, a wide hedge or an open ditch, may or blackthorn or a rambling rose, violets, primroses, old man's beard.

"Have you been to McCain's?"

"I haven't had that honour."

John looked down, as he always did when Jim put on his London manner. He said: "Once I took his harrow for a loan and I peekered in through a crack in the barn door. Do you know what I saw?"

"Farm machines?" Jim had no interest in the contents of Mr McCain's barn.

"Farm machines! Farm machines!"

The riddle was too much for Jim. "I give up, John."

"I saw Rolls-Royces. One after the other going back into the darkness. Must have been forty of them, at least eight longwise, and however many rows back. And you could smell them . . ."

"What did they smell like, John?"

"What did they smell like? They smelled like Rolls-Royces."

"Perhaps Mr McCain collects Rolls-Royces."

John looked at him in shock. Could the man truly be so innocent?

"Or maybe he doesn't like the district to know how much money he's made."

On the evidence of John's look, that was better.

One cold day, they laid the hedge on the lane. Jim had never done such work, which was both heavy and delicate. In minutes, he was crimson with blood, his hands punctured in a hundred places by the thorn, his cheeks striped with grazes, his arms on fire from slashing at the stems till there was just a sliver of green wood and the bough came down like a feather into his left hand. When he looked up, John was thirty yards to his right and looking at him. Jim straightened. He said: "I have nothing to prove, John." John went back to work.

John looked at the country in a manner that was new to Jim and which for want of a better word he thought of as medieval. For John, Brackshire was still commons, not yet enclosed or even disenchanted. Since the first day, he had never questioned Jim and showed no interest at all in his exploits or opinions. Yet, once in a while, he would use the phrase "I wonder", as in "I wonder how many folks there are that lies in Haze churchyard."

Jim did some simple mathematics.

"Twenty thousand, you would say?"

No doubt John could have multiplied a thousand years by twenty deaths per annum. It was as if he preferred such statements from another's mouth.

"And do they all lie together, hoggledy piggledy?"

"I think they do, John."

Jim made John tell him the names of the birds and trees. He learned it was Venus that rose each evening over the wheat. Those were jackdaws that stood on the ewes' backs picking out with their beaks the softest wool for their nests. Jim did not understand why he was eager now to know things that he had been content for thirty years not to know. He supposed that he knew nothing of astronomy and botany because, as a Londoner, he needed to know nothing. His ignorance was purposeful. Was the same now true of his knowledge?

So the days elapsed amid the monotonous chink of songbirds. Pheasants strutted like peacocks between the daffodils. Rain drenched the cherry blossom which drifted against the verges as if it were spring snow. The bluebells died back. Oaks came into leaf and cow parsley into flower, and red campion, speedwell and forget-me-nots covered the hedge banks. Jim spent an hour watching house martins skimming flies off the wheat. Horse-chestnut candles gave a whiff of the suburbs. Poppies sprung up on the headlands.

There were times when Jim was at work, a certain posture as he drove in the fence posts, or heard the grain tinkle in the chicken trough, or pulled on his veil to tend the bees, or led the calf on her halter, or carried the pails of milk on his shoulder back to the house, when he seemed to himself a stranger. It was as if he were a figure in a picture or a character, not an important one, in an old film or television programme. These were sensations not so much of well-being, though Jim did feel well, as an uncustomary awareness of his arms or legs or neck or back: anyway, he thought, the nearest he would ever be to being happy. His hands were dirty and always grazed. Jim saw that for the first time since his travelling days, when he had worked at hard labour in hot sun, he was using his body for one of the purposes for which it had been made and that he was joining the main component of humanity, which still, and perhaps for several generations yet, laboured with the body. Jim remembered the Kurdish street porters in Mosul bent past the double under three or four hundred pounds of coffee or cement. The end of his business life in London, the story that went round and round in his recollection, no longer made him stand bolt upright in shame and humiliation. Here there was a style of British life, inarticulate and contented and withdrawn. Jim had passed out of the purview of the authorities and their incessant care for his well-being. He broke thirty public-safety ordinances before breakfast.

In this level country, Jim found he could see for miles. From the treehouse, he could make out, just above the intervening trees, the pepperpot tower and finial of some rich family's palace or folly and the spire of Brightwell light, ten miles away. Sometimes, on calm afternoons before the school run, he could hear the click and clatter of a branch-line train. He felt his horizons recede. For all his idleness and solitude, he seemed to be gaining in insight. At times, he felt he might achieve something at Paradise Farm, like his business but also quite unlike it, not commercial at all, nothing to do with money or fame or power or prestige, or with the self. Jim's imagination failed him. At night, he would sit sometimes on an iron bench with Argos between his knees, watching The Hunter rise and then set over the pasture. One night he saw the moon eclipsed, red as a butcher's apron, globular as he had never seen her, pitted with craters.

Jim did not like to go to bed. Often, he would take Argos for his walk at night. They would set off at sundown, amid new continents of clouds in the sky, and the tired murmurings of blackbirds. They passed through sleeping villages, setting off the halogen lamps of nervous householders, one by one, as if Jim were a celebrity in a blitz of press photographers. He felt that walking with a dog was proof enough that he was not a murderer. He carried a torch, but never used it. He followed the gleam of Argos' coat in the starlight. He could find his way home by lucid stars.

At first, Jim went only by the roads, and then by the public footpaths and bridleways, but, after a while, he took to the fields. Yet the ways he took, along The Maiden past the ford, skirting the church and the keeper's cottage in its clump of firs, seemed to him frequented, as if from the time when people went on foot. Before streams, Argos would wait for him, agleam in the starlight; and once he stood, one paw raised, by a sort of trench, recently dug, that looked like nothing so much as the holes the grave-robbers used to make in the olive yards around Paphos in Cyprus.

Jim liked the way time passed and an event — a pair of geese overhead or the sound of car doors and laughter outside a public house — became, as the light faded, as distant as the Congress of Vienna. In the gloaming, he felt less solitary, not so much from Argos glimmering just at the extremity of vision, but as if some other soul were also about in the small hours. Jim told himself that that made no sense. If he came upon nobody during his walks in the day, how much less so at three in the morning! There were not even poachers now that pheasants were two a penny.

Jim became wary. At times, he would stop of a sudden, to catch the sound of a step or the break of a twig. Once he heard, from Ladies Wood, the roosting pheasants begin to chime and clatter when he was half a mile away. It was not Argos who had disturbed them, for the dog was a-bristle at Jim's feet. Jim understood that even before he had learned properly to see, he must now learn to hear. He must stand for half an hour on the edge of a wood, casting up and removing the sounds of the bypass, or a woodcock groaning through the wood, or the thump of a rave from somewhere over the other side of Brightwell. He sensed that this person, whose only evidence was in sound, was wary of him. The person had no routine or pattern. Unlike Jim, who never trespassed, the person seemed to pass at will through houses and gardens.

"Who is it, Argos?"

Argos, who would bark at the sound of the train six miles away, seemed indifferent to the sound.

"Well, if you're not bothered, I'm not bothered."

Jim's old career, with its pageant of airport lounges and City boardrooms and its incessant decisions, now seemed to him quite out of scale. He felt that what he was looking for was not large or distant or loud, but small and near and overlooked, and would be revealed only to the most intense concentration.

This uneventful life was interrupted by an invitation to dinner at Mount Royal House, former seat of the Earls of Bolingbroke and now one of the principal residences of Charles and Marina Lampard.

CHAPTER
FIVE

The War Between the Toffs and the Chavs

The double door was opened by a manservant in a black suit. Like the men stationed in the park and by the obelisk, he looked at Jim with contempt. He spoke into his short-wave radio, then took Jim's topcoat and threw it onto a chair. Had the man been in livery, breeches, buckles and a powdered wig, he could not have treated the garment with more honest disdain. Across the flagged hall, which rose to the height of two rooms, a young woman was standing on her own, done up to the nines.

"Mrs Lampard?"

Jim clattered across the hall and put out his hand, which the woman looked at but did not take. Jim lowered the pitch of his approach.

"I am Jim Smith. It was kind of you to invite me."

She looked at him without acknowledgement. Round her throat was a necklace of blue diamonds.

"I hope the things arrived in one piece. If you don't mind, I asked John Walker and he thought you might wish to have them."

The woman waved her fingers. Jim could not tell what had displeased her: John Walker, the children's toys and the dog cart, or the mention of such items in the entrance hall of Mount Royal House. Were not the interminable drive through the gloaming, the obelisk, the ice-house and the lake, the idling vehicles where the avenues crossed, the house appearing and reappearing through the oaks, were those not enough to drive such insignificant objects out of his mind? In which case, why had she invited him to dinner? It could not be that she wanted Jim on visiting terms.

Mrs Lampard turned without speaking.

Jim followed her swishing dress through rooms lit from table lamps and the lights over paintings of eighteenth-century cities — Calcutta, Canton, Tellicherry — that filled him with a species of simple yearning. Everything was spotless and neat, as if the house and its contents were for sale. Jim suspected that the furniture and pictures conveyed information about the Lampards, about their station in life, their wishes and their friends, but he was not man of the world enough to unravel it. It occurred to him that he had passed his life deaf and blind to the signals of fashion.

Jim found himself thinking like Harriet Woodman. So Charles Lampard has found somebody who knows how to spend his money! He had a thought which another man might have turned into an aphorism: Without women, there is no purpose to money.

In a long room at the end, a group of people stood before high windows in attitudes of unease. This room, too, was of double height, and the guests looked particulate and solitary. Among them was Harriet herself, who made no sign of recognising Jim. Names and surnames came in one ear and went out the other, and with the last introduction, Mrs Lampard withdrew from Jim as if scorched.

"Do you shoot?" asked Harriet's husband. He spoke so loud that Jim thought perhaps he might be deaf.

"Now you live in that perfectly hideous house!" said a woman. She had a voice that would have quarried granite.

"No," Jim said and smiled at both. "I have come to live at Paradise Farm."

"Where?"

"Paradise Farm. He's moved to Paradise Farm."

A second couple unglued itself and moved towards the novelty. They were called Dark. He wore an elegant striped suit. She displayed enough of her bosom for Jim to regret that she did not display more.

"Darling, this chap's moved to Paradise Farm."

"I never really cared for Paradise Farm," said Mr Dark.

The newcomers slid away.

A butler elbowed through with a tankard of champagne.

"Careful!" the lady bellowed. She dabbed at her dress of engine-green silk. It occurred to Jim that the clumsy butler was no professional servant, any more than the footmen at the door or the bullies in the park. Jim adjusted his expectations for dinner.

"I'll put you on my charity list. Name?"

"Do I look so very poor?"

"What?"

Jim thought best to start again. He shouted: "I'm afraid, sir, I only shoot pistols."

"Targets."

"Yes."

Mr Woodman looked down at Jim kindly. "When I was at school, I wanted to give up shooting, and both my grandfathers called me in and both said the same thing. Tim, they said, I advise you to think very carefully. If you give up shooting, you'll find your middle years weighing very heavy on your hands."

Jim did not shoot game, ride, climb, sail or dance, and his middle years were still before him. Such philosophy was premature. Harriet was beckoning to her husband. Jim allowed himself to slip away.

He stood before a handsome man who had on his face a look of calm satisfaction. Around him and, so to speak, at one step or even two steps below in rank, were several women. Could this be the famous Charles Lampard?

"We were just talking about Japan. Have you visited Japan?" There was an insolence to the question, as if he were reluctant to share his harem with a younger male.

"Many times," said Jim.

Jim's answer irritated the man. As he proceeded with his tale, which was about the temples at Kyoto, at each interval he deferred to Jim with phrases such as "as our friend knows better than I do". Even when he had crossed the China Sea, had passed through the skyscrapers of Shanghai, entered the Forbidden City and navigated the Three Gorges, he would turn and say: ". . . as this gentleman will explain". Jim felt in the wrong, less for having visited Japan than for confessing his visits. He had never taken a holiday, and perhaps held holidays in smaller respect than they deserved. He sensed animosity, tempered by their natural generosity, from the women about him. Also, and sotto voce, Jim wondered how this booby could have founded Lampard Trust, turned a down-at-heel haulage business into the greatest industrial conglomerate in Europe, extracted half a billion dollars in fees from the forced liquidation of American Tool, sold Multimix Foods for fifty times its revenues.

A woman leaned against Jim and whispered: "H. chucked."

Jim started from the touch of Mrs Dark's bosom on his upper arm.

"Who is H.?"

She looked at Jim, and then up and over his head to the distant ceiling. "Who indeed!" she murmured.

It was as if they, that is, Jim and she, had no need of H., whoever he or she might be.

There was a commotion by the double door. A short, burly man of about fifty-five or sixty had walked into the room. He gave the impression of having come from some business of importance to which he would soon return. In the intervening time, his young wife's guests had his complete attention. They lined up like schoolchildren.

Seeing the Lampards under the same ceiling, Jim understood better the economy of their marriage. It seemed to Jim that to a thug such as Lampard, with his thousands of millions in money, women were luxuries for public consumption, as hounds and horses and carriages had been for Mr Woodman's two grandfathers. Marina Lampard was young and, as much to the point, capable, as every item in the room showed. That she could choose her owner, unlike those hounds and horses, and had selected Lampard could only raise that man in the esteem of onlookers. That she had chosen to remain his private possession and not, like other beautiful women of modern times, sought the admiration of millions on television or the internet or magazines, was a further confirmation of his masculinity. It was as if each were a mirror to the other's self-regard, reflecting each other's face and fortune back and forth, in a darkening enfilade, till they passed into infinity. Yet, something in this marriage of January and May stuck in Jim's eye and seemed to speak only of a mercenary exchange of services at an agreed valuation. He could not imagine an overmastering passion at its foundation. He supposed Mrs Lampard had been brought up, not in a castle, nor yet quite in a cottage, with a sense of herself that could only be fully expressed in this profusion of power and expense.

Jim had passed a career in business without knowing anything of political economy, except a phrase of the Abbé Galiani that had stuck in the sieve that was his mind. Riches, this man had written, were not quantities that were fixed or certain, but a relation between two persons: *La ricchezza è una ragione tra due persone*. To a solitary man, property is valueless. It is only when another person wants his property that it becomes precious. And Mrs Lampard was precious, for else why would people want to steal her, and her children, wherever they were, and security men treated the dinner guests like criminals? If there was to her an air of authentic fear, well, then, Mrs Lampard must be in very great danger. She wore her diamonds, Jim thought, not to adorn her bare throat, but to protect it.

"I know you, don't I?" Lampard scoured Jim with his eyes.

Jim said: "I'm new to the district. I bought Paradise Farm."

"Yes," he said. Lampard's inquiry had ended, no doubt as often, on his own property. "You got it free."

His eyes passed from Jim to Mrs Dark and rested there; or did not rest, but passed from head to toe, and back to bust, to haunch, to bust, to head again. Mrs Dark struck the pose of an antique athlete, one foot ahead of the other, hand on hip. Lampard moved on.

Mrs Lampard stood in her rippling silk by the door, as if to indicate that the guests should pass through it. As they squabbled to be last through, it was plain to Jim that they were not the most honoured group of guests nor, equally, the least honoured, but stood somewhere on a scale that had its feet in the mire and its top somewhere elevated beyond his imagination. Beneath these distant ceilings there paced the leaden ghosts of prime ministers and financiers and film actresses and Continental princes. In inviting Jim and Harriet together, buyer and agent, Mrs Lampard discharged her social obligations wholesale. She slaughtered her guests, Jim thought, smiling at Tim Woodman as he passed through the door, in coveys.

Seeing Tim Woodman rigid across the table was poignant to him. Had Jim but known it, the man had given his life to excelling in sport, and had breathed in the praise of gamekeepers and land agents and seed salesmen, good but impressionable men. In a deep ravine with the birds scooting overhead, Tim Woodman was a god. Out of it, he seemed a poor person: deaf, angry, without conversation or gallantry, stony broke. As for Harriet Woodman, she was a woman of a sort Jim was now better educated to recognise: children grown up, frustrated with a husband who shot pheasants all winter and played golf all summer, and did not seem able to make money: indeed, at every moment of his life had put the cart before the horse. At first, her husband's fecklessness had flattered her femininity, for she liked to be a woman and of use. It appeared to her now in a different light.

In his different occupations, Jim had never learned that the country, rather than the city or its suburbs, was the refuge of an accurate view of the world. He supposed that what had begun as a distraction had overrun an entire way of life, and pastimes such as fox hunting and pheasant shooting had become the chief business of existence. It was as if some mysterious core to this way of life had vanished, leaving just the shell of its recreation. What that original purpose was, Jim could not say but it obviously had to do with property and power and women, for all things did. The perverse result was that these men were forever recuperating though from what was not evident, unless it was from their own recuperation. Jim pulled himself together. Don't be such a stuck-up prig, Jim Smith! Had he been told that but for three years in the army, which he had discharged playing polo in Chipstable, Tim Woodman had passed his life without a single hour of labour, and yet felt himself much put upon, Jim would not have believed it.

Mrs Lampard gestured to her left, and Jim stood while she seated herself. Opposite him was Mr Dark, who, as far as Jim could judge, was a lawyer. He had that air of secret wisdom that never failed to discomfort Jim. Whenever Jim had needed to consult such practitioners, they were never there, or rather had slipped into some maquis of jurisprudence from which they would descend on Jim's projects with acts of reckless sabotage. Jim was a bundle of the usual prejudices, and lawyers were outdone in his disapproval only by stockbrokers and private bankers.

Dark's wife howled at being separated from her husband. She was dragged off to sit by Lampard. Her bare shoulders and thrust-up bosom made Mrs Lampard look girlish, even tedious. Beyond the Woodmans sat a lady, ramrod-straight and martyred, as if done to death by her placement. Jim wondered if H.'s chucking, whoever H. was, had disturbed the arrangement of the table and left this lady to bear the consequences. In which case, she was no doubt a familiar of Mrs Lampard, perhaps even her mother. And booby was her father. Beyond them, the guests vanished into obliteration.

At Jim's back was a sensation of twilight. He turned to his hostess and wondered whether he could say: I've turned your fine garden at Paradise Farm into a sheep-walk. Jim had no knowledge of fashionable women, and no small conversation. He preferred women such as Mrs Dark, whose every movement spoke only to his masculinity, who demanded, for her own reinforcement, a masculine tribute. Her gesture spoke to every man in the room: Why do you fuck these insipid women when you can fuck me! Jim could not speak to the trembling divinity beside him.

Who would not look at him.

It seemed to Jim that it was not possible to approach Marina Lampard without threat, and without being questioned by one of the employees concerned with her security. She was not a person that one might come on in the next seat in an aeroplane, or on The Hard at Brightwell, or at the popcorn counter of the Odeon in the interval of a performance. Either she avoided such places or came to them only once they had, in some fashion, been made safe: as a private charter or private party she had herself selected, invited, assembled and paid for. Such exercises in control (of others and, who knows, herself) must have occupied her time and exhausted her energy, for she gave no sign of ever having been at leisure. Jim tasted his wine, which was quite savourless. For all his unworldliness, he could see that even this giant house, this machine for making people stare, was itself just a hotel in a life that flitted between . . . where? And where? Fort Austin? Porto Achille? St-Etienne? Jim knew nothing of such places.

He remembered Lord Bolingbroke in his wine cellar, and thought him hospitable, though poor.

Such a woman as Mrs Lampard must, it seemed to Jim, be wearisome to persons of an independent spirit. He looked about him at the other guests. They appeared content enough, either because they liked to be private property, or because they existed by general rules that were not altered by any peculiarities of temper or circumstance. They were eager, with their smiles at host and hostess, to help the Lampards complete an edifice of sexual happiness that approached perfection. Or were they, thought Jim, stunned by the Lampards' fortune, as by a blow to the head?

Yet Jim was seated in the place of honour at the mistress' left while she stared down the candlelit table. In the flicker of the white tapers, she was a-tremble. She had brown eyes that seemed to be turned inward, as if she had no interest in anything but herself. Jim could not imagine her ever having smiled or laughed or kissed anything but her own mouth in the mirror. Close up, she seemed too young to bear the weight of all this luxury and ostentation. Rather, Mrs Lampard was like a young girl who dresses sometimes this way and sometimes that, not being quite sure of her own nature. She had that dazed look that Jim had seen before in fine women, assaulted by admiration as if by artillery.

"I have John Walker working for me." Jim's first mention of John in the hall had produced nothing, but he had no other gambit to deploy.

"I was brought up," said Mrs Lampard, "never to listen to gossip."

There was a hint of declamation in her tone, as if she imagined that someone other than Jim were listening, or as if she had said to the mirror before coming down: Always be Mrs Charles Lampard! Never not be Mrs Charles Lampard!

Well, lucky old you, thought Jim. What was the gossip of the villages about John? That he drank? And hurt himself putting out a fire in the baler? That he had once been found walking with May Denny when she was still in Miss Carrow's class? That he was the last person to see your unfortunate predecessor, Jean Lampard, at 8 a.m on the day, 11 August, 1967, as he repaired the cutter bar on his tractor? That he found her mare entangled in its reins beside Ladies Wood and, instead of going straight to Jim Morris at the police house in Haze, had walked the horse home and unsaddled and washed and fed and watered her?

Be Mrs Charles Lampard! Say nothing out of the ordinary, for it dates and places you! Say nothing at all!

". . . and then with his left hand caught it. Old Bolingbroke made him a silver plate with the date, and the name of the stand, and an engraving of the woodcock."

These fragments of sporting recollection fluttered down the table like paper. Mrs Lampard turned away. Her interest in Jim was so faint that he felt there was no purpose to his being there.

He turned, as he had learned in London, to his left-hand neighbour and found the lady in green available for conversation.

"Would you kindly remind me of your name?"

"Glory. Glory Gainer," she shouted. "I suppose I talk to you now, do I? Golf, is it?"

"Excuse me?"

"Weekender?"

"No. I'm at Paradise Farm."

"Horrid smoky house."

"It doesn't seem so to me."

"Well, it wouldn't, would it?"

She looked at Jim as a teacher might a disappointing pupil.

She sighed. "The county used to be just so nice."

"It still is."

"It was just so nice. Before you came."

Mrs Gainer was precise in her articulation, and the main force of her voice fell on "before", not on "you". It was not that Jim had ruined the district. Jim was neither here nor there. It was more that Brackshire had been a sort of Garden of Eden which must now make place for the Jims of this world. Jim wondered if Mrs Gainer had ever heard herself speak.

"Such a pity," she murmured. "Such a great pity."

"Why a pity?"

"Gentlemen, sir."

Jim must have looked interrogatory, for she continued: "I mean for all I know you may be a good chap, but you are not what we call a gentleman."

Jim was less insulted by Mrs Gainer's statement than perhaps he should have been. Having brought himself up and never circulated in what is called society, Jim may have lacked some of those graces that, taken as a whole, comprised Mrs Gainer's ideal of a gentleman.

Or was there in him an absence of something which, it being an absence, Mrs Gainer could not put her finger on? In deciding to do some one thing rather than another, Jim acted not out of habit or custom, or to be praiseworthy to his neighbours, but in a secret aversion to the smallest dependency. If Mrs Gainer had known that Jim prized independence beyond anything, she might have been kinder in her judgement.

Jim thought it unlikely that he would be invited among these people again. Yet he did not throw off his boots and pull open his collar, take a bottle by the neck and Mrs Lampard by the waist, nor could a sympathetic eye have noted even the slightest slackening of his attention to his neighbours. It was rather as if he wished to leave a complete impression of himself before he cleared the stage, like the clothes of a suicide folded on the shingle.

"Shot with Jack once years ago. Carried his cartridges in a lady's handbag."

That was Tim Woodman. Jim thought that the story was not true, but had become so in the telling.

"The thing was, he was a bloody good shot. I remember . . ."

"Of course, he was, you big pig. Otherwise he'd carry his cartridges in a pigging cartridge-belt. My father used to say: If you want to do embroidery, you need at least a V.C."

These phrases had no more meaning to Jim than hieroglyphs. As a style of conversation, however new and strange to him, it had the advantage that it required no great exertion.

"Well, he has Markie Neal's *Venus in a Groovy Hat*, which must be worth a penny."

Dark checked himself. Jim understood that the man, for all his worldliness, was no familiar of the Lampards or of this company, and nor was his hard-working wife. The man was clever enough to judge that it was possible, even expected, to speak lightly of Lord Bolingbroke, but not of a work of self-conscious art; and that a picture of a sensationally pretty woman, wearing nothing but a hat in the style of thirty years ago, by a painter dead of the complications of Aids was too much of a good thing that, in general, should consist of one partridge in flight or, better, a brace against snow. It had not yet occurred to this man — but it would, alas, it would — that the subject of the picture had a name and for part of the time that name had been Jean Lampard.

To help him out, Jim said: "I saw lovely things when the Bothy was open to the public."

The man swept aside Jim's outstretched hand and splashed his own way to the conversational shore. "You're quite wrong. It's all rubbish."

Jim was suddenly weary of his neighbours, with their baffling preoccupations and strange courtesies. Their ideas seemed to him mere clutter, or like cobwebs that had lost their spiders, but still swung and glittered in the morning sunshine. He had resolved to have no more to do with these fine people, to whom he was linked only by situation, had not he turned and seen the present Mrs Lampard staring ahead of her. Jim looked up the table to see Mrs Dark wriggling beside

Charles Lampard, but that was not what she was looking at. Behind her frigidity were the relics of fright.

"This girl needs a plate!"

"You put your fucking hands elsewhere, Charles Lampard."

"Simmons! Give this girl a plate. Or I'll fire you."

Jim looked back at Mrs Lampard. Hard luck, ma'am, thought Jim kindly. I think if you marry a man for his money, you pay, over and over and over again.

She turned her face to Jim. There were ugly splashes of rage and shame on her cheeks. Jim was overcome with mortification, as if he had spoken out loud. Then she turned away. Jim thought: What do I know about it, ma'am? I know nothing about nothing.

"What H. feels is that Jack doesn't seem to have done anything about it." Dark appeared unaware of what was passing between his wife and Mr Lampard fifty feet away.

"About what?" Jim said, to encourage him.

"What do you think? Just to sit there, year after year, as your fields and house go to ruin and your money runs out, and not do anything about it. H. doesn't understand it."

Dark's change of tone to something more manly, plain and straightforward seemed to Jim no more honest than his urbanity. No doubt he was struggling for a manner that might work with his hostess. If that was his intention, he had no effect whatever on Mrs Lampard, who stared into space.

"Jack's unsound on hunting," said Glory.

72

Whether this was a product of a mind restricted in its interests or the last word in tact, Jim welcomed these changes in the conversational spirit. To prevent any reversion to Jean Lampard's portrait or the distressing scenes at the other end of the table, Jim replied. He felt that Mrs Gainer was severe on a man who had made a good impression on him. "Perhaps," Jim murmured, "Lord Bolingbroke's hunting days are over."

"What do you mean? You're an Anti, aren't you?"

Jim was very much in favour of hunting, only not at dinner. Lord Bolingbroke was blind. Jim now understood that, in Glory Gainer's opinion, that was not good enough. Sorting through the oddments of Brackshire conversation for Jim's purpose in life, she had thought to find it and she did not like it at all. Prudent as ever, Jim saw that any attempt to occupy his own position, a little towards the outside of the circle of Gainers and Woodmans, was as desperate as to hope to meet Mrs Lampard on a London bus. For the purposes of his companions at table, there were themselves and then barbarism. Beyond the park gates of Mount Royal House were shamans and steppes. Brightwell was Asia. It was now necessary for Jim, by a side-slip or hop, to rejoin the main stream of this society.

He was forestalled. Dark said: "He's perfectly entitled to his opinion, Glory. Don't be such a battleaxe."

Jim could not but admire the man's front. Dark's tactlessness about Lord Bolingbroke's picture was nothing to this larger offence of Jim's. *The man was opposed, on grounds of principle, to fox hunting!* Yet if

Jim were to step back or, rather, allow his mind to float on its fumes of meat and wine and Mrs Lampard's scent a little away from the table, he would see that this was all for the best. If, for example, Lord Bolingbroke had been the only Protestant in the district, then to draw attention to his peculiarity would have had consequences. Except to its devotees, what did fox hunting matter? He was glad that there was an occupation so healthy and sociable to absorb their vigour. Or did they know these things much better than Jim? Could it be that fox hunting was not a mere pastime, but a badge or emblem of a social condition so valuable that it could only be symbolised; and that for a class that had no other way of delimiting itself from the next, it was a matter of life and death? In that case, Jim thought, there was nothing contrary to social reason in Glory Gainer's evil glare.

Diversion came from where Jim had not expected it.

"Harriet Woodman tells me you had a fox at Paradise Farm."

Jim turned at Mrs Lampard. She was staring into the darkness as if she had not opened her mouth.

"Oh yes," said Harriet, who had sworn only Jim to secrecy. "We were . . ."

"So did you tell the huntsman? Did you?"

"I told the huntsman, Glory, that they might ride the hounds over Paradise Farm after harvest."

Mrs Gainer was dumbfounded. "So why the dickens are you an Anti?"

"Just leave him alone, Glory."

74

"Why should I? That's what I hate about these bloody Antis. They don't even have the courage of their own convictions."

Jim did not feel it would be possible, with what remained of the evening and the good nature of the guests, to unravel this tangle and set Mrs Gainer to rights. What mattered was Mrs Lampard. Why can't she let go of Paradise Farm? Why must she have everything, like whoever it was in the Bible? Was that the reason he was seated beside her?

"Harriet said you were in business."

Jim said: "I used to have a company that wrote financial software. We had a product that allowed the High Street banks to know how much money they had and how much they owed at any second of the day or night. For a time, we had a monopoly. Somebody in the City told me we needed to expand and for that we needed capital. I believed him. At least, I floated the company on the stock market. A mistake, as it turned out. I was found to be unneeded."

The subject was painful to Jim and made no impression on his hostess, who did not appear to be listening. He tied the loose ends of the conversation with an honest truth. "I'm no businessman. For a while, I was able to write simple computer code."

Mrs Lampard did not turn to him. She said: "I'm learning ancient Greek."

Her neighbours recoiled as if from a serpent. It had not occurred to them that Charlie Lampard had married a swot. In the least bedroom in the furthest wing of the airy palace of the Lampards' good fortune,

75

a piece of ceiling plaster fell and broke into a thousand pieces.

"What the devil for?"

"To help Sophy."

Beside Mrs Lampard was a little girl in a white nightgown. Jim had had little to do with children, but he would have put the girl at about six years of age. The brutality of the father and the affectation of the mother were either abolished or not yet manifest. Her hair fell to the small of her back. It occurred to Jim that it had never in her life been cut. He supposed that Marina Lampard had consented to bear one child but on the condition that she be a British *infanta*: that she be sad and insomniac and frightened; that she be her mother in miniature as in those dark and dirty pictures at the Bothy. She, too, would be the spoiled and timid bride of some businessman in need of dusky trophies for his houses. The little girl was looking at Jim as if she meant to murder him. It seemed to Jim that children, before they have learned the conventions of adult society, give vent to their parents' secret enmities.

"You're the man who lives in our house."

"Sophy!"

For all her rebuke, Mrs Lampard did not seem displeased at her daughter's impertinence. The child was an aspect of her vanity. To have sold Jim Paradise Farm for money was an act of sufficient condescension; but to introduce him, free and unmerited, into the family circle, was grace. Jim said: "I am the man, Sophy. That doesn't mean you can't come with your friends whenever you want."

"It's not the same."

"I know." Jim felt sorry for the child and the upheavals of her life. He said to himself: You can have it back, young lady. I won't be here for ever, or even very long.

"Sweetheart!"

That was Lampard. The top end of the table had turned as one to look at the novelty and were smiling at Sophy with the warmth of cotton wool. Mrs Dark had her arms open wide, as if to show that along with everything else she "did", she also "did" maternity. It was as if the child were a supplementary course of food, a sorbet or a dish of *îles flottantes*, to be spooned off a plate. As Sophy Lampard skipped the length of the table, the door beyond her opened.

It was a door to a pantry or butler's room: the place from which the waiters and food had come and to which they had disappeared. Yet the door that opened opened not on mahogany and linen and green felt, but on another place, to which Jim could not give a name, only that it was a place that was familiar to him and he must once have inhabited. An orphan grey light came in through the door, like a false dawn when the cock crows and the first dogs bark. Jim was certain at once that two orders of reality had intersected, and that this was not providential nor under his control, nor available to the other mortal persons in the room. There was no break in the talk. The little girl continued towards the head of the table. Emilia Dark shivered and allowed Lampard to smother her shawl about her shoulders. Glory Gainer glared. It occurred to Jim that this was the moment of his death, and he felt regret because something — he did not know what, but to do with his new life in the country or this evening — had begun to interest him in living. He breathed out and breathed in again.

Across the open boards by the wall, beyond the outer edge of the French carpet, Jim heard a step. It was light, but neither hurried nor uncertain. He thought it might be a woman's bare foot. He stared into the hissing gloom by the window. The heavy curtains billowed as if the tall woman stepping there had drawn a hand or some pointed implement across them. Jim breathed out and breathed in a second time. He thought to hear the step on the carpet. The child had stopped just short of the end of the table. It seemed to Jim that the colossal figure by the window was pointing something at the child.

Jim stood up. If he had any intention, it was to interpose himself between the windows and the child. As he stood up, he realised that he had not the strength to carry out his intention. An obstacle stood between him and the child. It was an obstacle of the nature of stone or steel, but it was not in the object world. It was in himself. It was fear, of course, of death and injury and loss, and of something far more comprehensive. It was fear that all his knowledge was false because the world was not as he had been told. Chaos engulfed him. At the table, candlelight and puzzled eyes sparkled and smeared. He imagined he had only a moment more to live, but death would not deliver him. Indeed, death was already on him. He felt a sort of vertigo, but in reverse, a terror not of falling but of rising; and that yearning of the cliff edge to be through with it all, even at an unspeakable cost. He heard the step on the carpet. The curtain at the next window billowed and subsided; then the next; then the two last. The door at his end of the room opened on the same evil glimmer. And closed. Sophy Lampard climbed on Emilia Dark's lap.

Jim breathed out.

Tim Woodman's face was full of kindness. "Are you all right, old boy?"

"I didn't mean it," said Glory, looking away. She was, perhaps, not accustomed to being listened to or for her words to have an effect. "Actually, my daughter and her partner are Antis, bloody fools."

Jim could not speak. He patted Mrs Gainer on the hand.

Jim sat down. He opened his mouth. He tried to speak.

Jim felt Mrs Lampard stand up. He rose again, but she had turned her back and was leading the child and the women out of the room. Jim had read of females leaving the dinner table in a body, but never thought to witness it. He needed to be alone, not to be offered a cigar from a box or listen to Lampard teasing his father-in-law or Richard Dark making a packet from building on the Common at Witchbourne. The alternative, on his right side, was Tim Woodman wildfowling in Siberia. Jim resolved to be less prodigal of his sympathies in future. He would have given his life to have Glory Gainer booming beside him like a dredger in the Bristol Channel.

Jim thought: There are no laws to science, nor to good behaviour, merely gestures in the dark, ghosts, arbitrary essences, inane customs. Truth and falsity are just names, for something can be turned into its reverse by some fancy or caprice of the dark. Nothing we do or say has the remotest value or makes the smallest sense or extends beyond the instant of its action or saying.

"The man fucking sent me up the wall. He was absolutely the worst kind of old-fashioned, British, stick-up-your-arse, hands-on manager, who wanders round picking up pennies off the carpets."

Yet even in Jim's utter helplessness, where the foundation of all his actions and thoughts had been demolished, where all his upbringing was suddenly so much wasted time, there was something else, that sudden relish or taste for life, that had run through his heart like a spear and left a taint of exhilaration, or what might even have been termed pleasure.

"He was so fucking mean, there were no stock options, no incentives, no expenses, no nothing. No way could he attract or retain motivated staff. He didn't even have a fucking overdraft. The whole business was run from its cash flow. And always fucking re-inventing the wheel. Everything had to be in-house: research, finance, sales, even the payroll."

Jim felt, at the very moment that he must set out towards destination terror, that he had found or been given some means to assist him, like a suit of armour or a repeating pistol. In his euphoria, he said to himself:

Well, Jim Smith, did you think you were going to live for ever?

"What happened to him?"

"The City wouldn't take the stock unless he was got rid of. He was bought off. I can't remember how. Fucking lucky to sell out when he did. Quit business, I think."

Jim came back to earth. At the table, the men were in a cluster round Lampard. Though smaller than any man at the table, his fame and fortune seemed to enlarge him. The men lounged or smoked in postures of exaggerated ease. They had not heard Jim fall back to earth.

Jim spoke. "Who are you talking about?"

Lampard was bored. He was bored of his wife's dinner party, bored of her guests, bored even of making fun of her father. His new favourite had tripped off with the ladies, trailing her shawl. He was bored of talking to these clowns.

"Smith, was it? Jones? I saw there was nothing to be gained from meeting him."

Lampard stood up. By the time the men returned to the main drawing-room, their hostess had retired. The guests were dismissed. Jim said indiscriminate farewells and drove home, his shirtfront still gleaming from the evening party at Mount Royal House.

CHAPTER
SIX

Duties of the Still-Room Maid

As Jim picked his way through his pasture, his car headlights picked up an oddity. Through the drizzle, a ewe was staring at a trembling lamb as if it had nothing to do with her. The lamb looked like a new-born soul. Jim's first thought was to drive on, back to the house and then go to his bed, and perhaps that would have been better. Instead, he parked his car, woke Argos, put on his overall, found sackcloth and a bottle of iodine, lit a hurricane lamp and hung it on a post, and began to towel cold yellow slime off the lamb. He imagined the lamb had been born not an hour earlier, as he sat at table with the Lampards. He pushed his finger into the lamb's mouth and found it cold. The ewe continued to regard them with surprise. When Jim tried to catch her, she galloped off.

In the end, Jim caught and upended the ewe. She had milk on both sides. He put the lamb to the teat. With what little strength it had, it forced itself back. It was as if the thick yellow colostrum were poison to it. The ewe struck at Jim with its hooves until he sat on her. In the end, he put a halter on the ewe and dragged her and carried the lamb into the byre.

Jim sat in his overall in a chair in the kitchen, an alarm clock beside him on the kitchen table. Every two hours, he went down to the byre, caught and upended the ewe, milked her into a jug and then filled a syringe. The lamb swayed on its feet in the straw. He dared not feed her by stomach tube. If by some mischance he put the tube in her lung, she would not have the strength to cough it out. He squirted 10 millilitres of the colostrum through the side of her mouth. It foamed round her teeth and dripped down. At 4 a.m., he wondered if it were perhaps kinder to let things run. At 6 a.m., he went down, full of foreboding. The ewe was standing with a look of incomprehension. The lamb was stiff in the straw.

Jim took himself off, but it was as if he could not leave the scene. In the morning light, another ewe was pawing the ground and grinding its teeth at the sky. The lamb, when it came, was sound and eager to feed. As it nuzzled into its mother's haunches, the ewe turned, and turned, and turned.

"Stay still, you daft animal."

Jim decided to act. He would give this lamb enough colostrum through the stomach tube to keep it alive through the day. If the ewe still rejected it, Jim would bottle-feed it to weaning, so help him.

Jim was warming the lamb on the stove in the kitchen and did not want to answer the telephone. He let it ring and ring and then, exasperated, wrapped the lamb in sackcloth and picked up the receiver.

"Please," he said, interrupting a woman from Lampard Trust. "I'm unfortunately tied up now." For good measure, he added: "Also, while I'm about it, would you kindly say to Mrs Lampard that if she has business with me will she contact me in person rather than through her husband's employees? Thank you. Goodbye."

Jim hung up on the astonished functionary, only to see Rose glaring at him. She had a way of being around when anything happened. Her face said: Ye're an idiot, Jim Smith. Only an idiot messes with Charlie Lampard.

"So how was dinner at the Hall?"

Jim understood that Rose was a snob. She was bored by his solitude and thrift. She would have preferred it if he had been a rock musician, and she could fuss and scold each morning through a clutter of champagne bottles, bent needles and sleeping prostitutes. He said: "Is there anything you don't know, Rose?"

The bachelor blandishment disgusted Jim. He did not like gossip any more than his hostess of the night before.

Rose's answer let him off the hook. "That would be telling."

Jim poured out and, with reluctance, drank a last cup of coffee and got up. With her back still turned over the sink, Rose spoke up. No doubt her information was like farm milk and would not keep.

"I knew that girl when she had dirty knickers. She and her airs!"

Jim said nothing.

"They took Marina out of Miss Carrow's class, packed her off to the high school and then Oxford University. If you asked me . . ."

Jim had not.

". . . Mrs High-and-Mighty had only one thing on her mind for Pretty. And it wasn't a secretary course."

She looked at Jim and then turned back to her washing up.

"Well," said Jim, "it's a beautiful house."

"Oh yes, only the best for Charles Lampard." Jim saw that Rose approved of Lampard, but not of his wife. Money was like an electric current that could alter polarities, and turn what would be a vice in a woman into a virtue in a man. Jim had had enough of local celebrities.

"Would you like to help tube the lamb, Rose?" he asked.

"Oh no," she said, and scurried off. Jim understood that Rose, like a true countrywoman, hated anything to do with the old way of things. Outside the scullery, where Jim had set up his infirmary, the house linen was heaped in drifts. It was as if Rose absolutely refused to enter any room that contained needles and a sharp box and feeding bottles swimming in hypochlorite solution.

With infinite care, Jim began to push the tube into the lamb's mouth. She began to suck on it, and it went down easily. Jim injected 150ml of artificial colostrum down the tube and slowly drew it out. The lamb was asleep. He carried her in his arms down to her mother, who was whinnying and pawing the ground before its second lamb, which lay wet and dead on the ground.

Argos looked baffled. Jim, who never wept, felt like weeping. From a third ewe, a leg was protruding.

"Stay where you are, my darling. I just need to see what's happening."

Jim washed his hands and spread them with antiseptic gel. He felt the protruding leg. The ewe heaved, but nothing budged.

"Front leg or back leg? That's the question."

Jim couldn't find a head. He felt the leg up to the joint and realised it was a back leg.

"It's back to front, my love. I'm going to have to find the other leg, or both you and the lamb will die."

Jim felt as if he were crawling into a lightless cave. The ewe groaned. He found the tail, and the second leg, bent up against the belly. He tried to hook it back with the tip of his little finger. It was no good. The ewe groaned again. With all his strength, he pushed the lamb back into the womb and turned the foot, which appeared in the opening. When he tried to pull on the legs, his fingers slipped on the fatty, greasy wool.

Casting around, Jim saw some orange binder twine on the barbed wire. He made a slip knot and tied it round the fetlock, and pulled, and pulled. The ewe heaved. The legs came out to the hock, then tail, then haunch and shoulders, and then all in a great, wet heap.

"I did it! I did a breech birth! There is nothing I cannot do."

Jim picked up the lamb by the hind legs and swung it up and down. Then he put it down. The ewe sniffed at its face. The lamb was dead. Jim squatted in the dust, amid jackdaws and afterbirth. His overall was stained with blood and meconium and mud. He stank of animal.

John Walker turned up at noon in a state, as they say in Ireland, of having drink taken. He took one look at the animal in Jim's arms, and said: "Didn't I say you had to use the tube at once?"

"I did. She had 80 mil of synthetic colostrum within half an hour of my finding her. Look, John, there's no shortage of milk. The lambs just won't suck."

John glared at him. "Let's get her in the byre."

"She died with a full stomach," he said. "Feel."

John laid the body in the manger. He looked as perplexed as the lamb's mother. He said: "I mean you lost maybe one or two but . . ." Jim wondered if John Walker might be a superstitious man and did not want to be more precise.

"Maybe it was the ram Boynton used? Or maybe we didn't feed the ewes up enough towards the end?"

John was still shaking his head.

Jim summed up his morning's work. "Six doubles. All premature. All dead-born or weak or rejected by their mothers. All dead." The scale of Jim's defeat crushed him.

John turned on him. "You're bad luck, you are."

"By the way, John. Where do you go in the middle of the morning?"

That was contemptible. Jim at once regretted it.

"I do my work," John said, looking down.

"I know you do. It's none of my business." Jim never blamed employees, and was not going to start now.

John kept his head down. He said: "The Bloody Bone."

But why, Jim wondered, do you go to the pub in the morning? There can't be any company except the barman.

Jim thought: Even the barman is company too much. He said: "As long as you put in your eight, that's all that I'm interested in."

"Apart from Show day."

"Of course, John, you may have the day off to take Bramble to the Brightwell Show."

Jim buried the lambs on his own. It took him two hours. He was weary as he had never been. He sat on the iron bench outside with Argos at his feet. Thoughts buzzed about his tired head like blow-flies in the sheep pasture. According to the website of the Department of Animal Health at the University of Otago in New Zealand, the average flock will lose 15 per cent of its newborn stock each lambing. On established and well-managed stations, the average loss is 12 per cent. Jim had lost 100 per cent. He felt struck down, harried and terrorised as if the apparition of the previous night had pursued him into the daylight. He felt as he had once felt as a young boy at the whipping end of fate.

So, he had seen a ghost. Many people had seen ghosts or at least could make up a ghost story to frighten children or strangers. Jim was no great believer in science, and it seemed to him unthinkable that the universe had been brought in its entirety within the rule of law, or that nature was akin to mathematics, in which two and two always made four, and a circle was always a circle, and a square always and never not a square. It was the habit of men and women to mistake the universe for their way of describing it, and to believe that they had discovered laws that, in reality, they had invented. The apparition at Mount Royal House broke no more laws of nature than the twelve lambs he had just buried abolished the observed rates of mortality on well-managed sheep stations. It was the laws that were defective.

What if there were no science, just a succession of particular cases? What if there were no principles of nature, only habitual conjunctions that people labelled cause and effect? What if there were no history, only the supposition that the past resembled the present, and the future would be more of the same? What if there were no self, just a compendium of sensations, impressions, wishes, fears, regrets?

Like many solitary people, Jim inhabited not nature but a world fashioned within nature by the imagination. To Jim, the mind was not a computer, but more like a desert or badlands, riddled with metaphor and crossed by fugitive images, harried by storms of passion and regret, boundless and unsafe. He had dreamed of a woman, first as pure femininity, an Eve in the Garden of Eden, and then decked out with certain worldly characteristics. Of those characteristics, he could say one thing. They arose without exception from his new life: the nude portrait of Jean Thinne in the entrance hall of the Bothy, the Latin from his upstairs lintels, the tasks of barn and field that were his daily occupation.

Yet the apparition he had seen and heard at Mount Royal House had been a figment not of a dream, but of Jim's waking imagination. She had been all but palpable, as if she were about to take form in the sensuous world. Her incarnation, if that is what it had been, was not complete in that nobody else had seen or heard her: not Mrs Gainer or Capt. Woodman, or the little girl, or Lampard or his father-in-law or the Darks or Mrs Lampard. It seemed to Jim that what hindered her from becoming visible was not nature, but her own pure will.

He had thought that two orders of reality had somehow collided, for reasons quite beyond his understanding. He had thought that such an occurrence was neither common nor unique, and impossible to provoke or stage. The reality in which the apparition had her existence was so terrifying that it could not be inhabited by the living. Yet, at an angle to it or crossing it was that euphoria or exhilaration that had given him the courage to stand up and try to interpose himself between the apparition and the child. That sensation was so intimate, so inextricably bound up with his notion of his self, that it seemed indistinguishable from his humanity, or rather his mortality.

Jim had endured an unusual upbringing. His father had been a petroleum engineer. After attending an industry conference in Edmonton, he was returning by way of Japan when his DC-8 crashed on landing at Tokyo. In the rear of the aircraft, he was one of eight survivors. The next morning, together with Jim's mother, he boarded a BOAC 707 for London which broke apart and crashed into Mt Fuji along with its 124 passengers and crew. There were no survivors.

After this catastrophe, it was not to be expected that Jim would give much of an ear to Christian doctrine or even a dispassionate atheism. When he heard of the manner of his parents' death, his solitude became for a while unbearable. In the holidays from his boarding school, he lived with his mother's sister and her husband, good people whose only fault — and that irremediable — was that they were not his father and mother.

Jim left his school that summer for reasons that seemed good at the time. Perhaps he wished to mourn his dead parents, and did not think that England was a suitable place. Was it worth reviewing those reasons fifteen years later? Jim was then fourteen years of age. Because it was then the fashion to travel eastwards, he went to Greece and then to Cyprus where, at the village of Paphos on the west coast, Jim built a house. He slept on the beach. Each morning before dawn, the site foreman woke him by tossing a pebble on to his sleeping bag. They worked for five hours and then ate a breakfast of cheese and olives and wine. The wine tasted of turpentine. Jim's first day's work — a structural concrete wall that would be concealed by brick — he none the less two weeks later demolished and, to the bafflement of foreman and gang, rebuilt. Jim received, at the price of a kiss, 85 drachmas a day.

Was the house at Paphos still standing? What it had meant to Jim was this: he was able to look after himself.

For no particular reason, he travelled eastwards. In Palmyra, he worked as an errand boy for the German Archeological Mission. For a while he was employed as an orderly at the Ibn Sina Hospital in Baghdad and suffered an injury that he felt himself fortunate to have survived. In Manipur, he was hired by merchants to carry cheques and foreign currency by taxi to Calcutta. It was then that he adopted the habit of wearing a weapon, which he had not been able to shake. Once in Dindigul, where he worked as a clerk for Indian Airlines, he had watched a young man pass on a moped with a girl in a pink sari side-saddle behind him, and had wished that he, too, one day, might have a wife. He told himself it was a sentimental moment, composed in equal part of 120 degrees of the thermometer, the fog of diesel and wood-smoke, pink satin, a pretty face that might not be pretty for long, a slim, bare waist that might not be ditto.

In Singapore, Jim traded foreign currencies. It was not until he stood, by his hire car, amid the concrete and rice of Yamanashi Prefecture that he understood the purpose of his ten-year journey. With the detours he had made, and the places he had half-settled, he had travelled twenty thousand miles. He could make himself understood in twelve or thirteen languages, and was master of seven. He was possessed of about one hundred and fifty thousand dollars in money. Not for love of profit, but to do something with the independence and hardiness he had acquired, he had composed, in his head, a business plan that required neither capital nor expertise nor any dealing with the public in general. He had missed a strike of British coal miners, three or four movements in popular music and two football world cups. The hard experience of his loss was forgotten in the difficulties he had encountered. Without at any time having grieved for his mother and father, Jim stood in the rice and raised his arm in farewell. Then he turned away from his parents' empty tomb and returned, by air, to London.

Argos burst into a howl.

"What is it, lad?"

In the distance, two figures were moving through the wheat. They were splashes of colour, as if dressed for a carnival. They treated Jim's wheat as if it were herbage and Paradise Farm their promenade. They had reached the stag-head oak and were standing in front of it. Two months before, Jim would have ordered them off his ground. Now, he set off towards them. As he approached, they took on detail. One of them clambered into the lower branches. A flash of white leg, and a certain agility, showed this was a girl. Her companion had on trousers in the colours of the American flag. He was photographing the girl in the oak. Jim saw the girl was shirtless, and stopped in his tracks.

For an instant, his farm was transformed. It had not occurred to him that his fields and trees might have a public existence, as a background to a fashion shot or soft pastoral pornography of an "artistic" character. It was as if his universe had lost its sovereignty and been revealed as somebody else's back lot. Argos had reached them. Jim followed on.

Jim said: "Hello. Will you please walk in the tramlines, or the corn will be crushed and won't grow?"

The man smiled as if to say: Corn!

Up in the fork in the tree, the girl seemed content to be looked at. It occurred to Jim that she might be just thirteen or fourteen years of age. Together, the pair seemed to exist outside the routines of the country, and also of the city or town, but yet wished to be admired. They had the character, both lurid and tough, of circus performers. Only the man's camera, which looked to Jim like a professional instrument that used old-fashioned light-sensitive film, linked them to the world of work and occupation. Beyond them and the hedge Jim saw a school bus of about forty years before parked on the verge of the lane. It had been painted by hand in a sort of dusty purple.

"So, you make bread out of this?"

Not even fourteen. She put on her T-shirt, but not out of modesty, not at all. Just as she was not as old as she acted, so the man was not as young as he pretended. Could it be that he really had experienced at first hand the hippy age, had set off travelling in the 1960s and had, after many detours, reached the end of the line, the Brack Country? As a couple or pair, it was as if Mr and Mrs Lampard, with their discrepancy in age, had been transported to Bohemia. For all the sunshine and bright colours, the couple struck Jim with the same unease as had the Lampards. What did the man have that appealed to a pretty young girl? Whatever it was, it was not his small, sharp eyes.

Two months ago, Jim would have said: You are trespassing. There is a public footpath over there. Yet there was something about the couple that held information of use to him. He sensed that they, like Mr Dark of last night, or H., whoever H. was, were pioneers of change in Brackshire.

"Do you want to come up to the house and have some tea or a drink?"

The man looked at Jim with infinite contempt. Jim recognised that he used the girl as a snare or net for men, though for what purpose Jim could not tell.

He said: "We came to see the tree."

"You came to see my oak tree?"

He shook his head. "Your tree!"

The girl said: "Why do you have to own everything? This tree belongs to the world."

This was not a line of conversation that Jim ever found rewarding. He said: "So, no tea."

"We'll take some bread."

"I'm afraid I don't carry bread in my farm clothes."

That night, a creature found its way into the hen house at Paradise Farm and killed every bird in it. Jim found the chickens in the morning, scattered in the straw or across the perches, decapitated or with their breasts open to the bone. Jim counted the birds and found not one had been taken away. He felt a momentary sympathy for Mrs Gainer and her campaign against the fox.

The pigs Jim saved by good husbandry. He knew Careless well enough to see that she was listless, and it must be a sick sow that is driven from her food by her young. He put his hand under the flap of her ear and found her scalding hot. Her teats were rimmed with red. Jim called the vet, who would not come, but left out for him on the step of the surgery in Brightwell two injections to be put straight into the teats. That was more easily said than done. Jim made a crush out of sheep hurdles, and the sow bent it as if it had been a dry-cleaner's coat-hanger. With a bucket of pignuts and some ingenuity, Jim enticed her into the angle made by a five-bar gate, pulled the gate tight to the fence and chained it shut, at which moment Careless accepted both defeat and the injections. By the next morning, sow and piglets were back on their food.

As for the bees, well, Jim thought, that could have happened to anybody. It was hot, and from the house he could hear a humming sound like a distant sawing. When he came up to the hive, the air was black with bees. Returning with his veil, Jim found them in a tight, hot ball in a hawthorn bush just coming into flower and leaf. Sweet as pie, not one tried to sting him through his glove or trousers. Jim brought up an empty hive and then sawed away the branch and laid it in front of the entrance to the hive.

Jim squatted on his heels and watched the bees. At first, in ones or twos they walked through the narrow entrance to the hive. It must have been satisfactory, for by darkness, they had all gone in. Jim put his ear to the hive and heard a humming that he mistook for contentment. The next morning, when he went to check on them, the new hive was empty.

Jim guessed that he had somehow failed to capture the queen, and they had swarmed after her at first light. What was strange was that the old hive, which held the remnant of the colony, had also swarmed and was quite empty.

John looked at him.

"It's right, John. These things happen. We think we know so much about everything, but we don't. People have been living with bees for thousands of years and still don't have a clue why they do one thing rather than another."

John did not believe him. "You're bad luck, you are," he said.

CHAPTER
SEVEN

The Field of Cloth of Gold

The day of the Brightwell Show dawned hot and blue as any could wish. Raising Argos and going down to the byre, Jim found John and the cow less calf had already set off. As he crept in the Show traffic along the Brightwell ring road, he forgot his bad luck and found himself drawn into a holiday spirit. The barley had been cut on each side of the road, and the new straw baled and stacked into blocks that shone in the sun like ingots of gold. The whole land was drenched in gold. In the distance, Jim saw snapping flags and blowing canvas and heard the echo of a loudspeaker.

Inside, men and women were shopping or lounging on the grass in the sunshine with paper cups of beer. What was for sale seemed to have no relation to Brightwell or Brackshire or the sunny day, but to have been assembled from all over the world. There were woollens from Ecuador and onyx bird-baths from Baluchistan. Out at the far extremity, Jim saw Mrs Gainer, harrying children and ponies over jumps. She waved violently. He proceeded down the wide avenues of the temporary town, past swimming-pool makers and sellers of four-wheel-drive vehicles, towards the sound of the public-address. The machinery fell away. Now there were men in neat sports jackets and women with hats and plastic goblets of champagne, tented estate agencies, solicitors' partnerships, sellers of pensions and life insurance, pavilioned banks each with its own automated teller machine, the constabulary, private schools. Some men wore straw hats, as if they were women, but not like women for the hats were all the same.

It seemed to Jim that the equestrian activities, and the game shooting, and the cows and sheep and pigs, and the dairy goats and alpacas, and the poultry and the caged birds had been driven to the boundary fence as if by an explosion in the midst of the showground or, rather, as pollen is scattered from the surface of water by a drop of oil. What that explosion was, Jim had not the experience or the insight to tell. All he could say was that it had to do with changes that had occurred elsewhere in England some years or even tens of years before.

Could it be that Brackshire, with its obstinate manners and overstocked past, was to be domesticated and disarmed? Brackshire would now join the mainstream of a country that had lots of money and not much to do. Jim's heart sank. Having always felt himself to be of the modern party in Great Britain, he was now out of sympathy. He felt he was being left behind, in thick weather, on a bad road.

On a lawn in front of an enclosure, in which young men in military uniform stood on their heads on motorbikes, Jim saw a tall gentleman with long white hair. About him there was an abstraction of manner that was not to be put down solely to his blindness, as if, in whatever unfolded before Lord Bolingbroke's mind's eye, there were not land agents and pretty women in hats, but desert cemeteries or rigging hung with ice.

"Lord Bolingbroke?"

"Who wants him?"

"Jim Smith."

"Ah. I hoped that you might be here."

He turned and took Jim by the arm. As at their first meeting, Jim felt himself the object of Lord Bolingbroke's attention. It was as if Jack had no friends or occupations or any past, but had been created that moment to be of service to Jim. His summer clothes, though not untidy, hung upon him like flags on a still day. Not well supplied with flesh, he now looked like a ghost in the costume of half a century before.

"You didn't come to call on me."

"I didn't know you were sincere."

Bolingbroke smiled. "I don't have time not to be sincere, Jim. Will you kindly take me to the barns?"

"Of course. John Walker is showing his cow."

"Ah! Who is getting cow and man home?"

Jim had given no thought to the matter. "I shall," he said.

"Thank you." Jack stopped. He said: "You think I am unkind to Marina in hanging that portrait in the hall."

It was as if the events of the past three months had not occurred, and they were back in Jack's wine cellar at the opening of spring. Jim had given no thought whatever to the feelings of the second Mrs Lampard. Since that evening party at Mount Royal House, he seemed to be for ever seeing her, bent at the waist to take a bouquet from a schoolgirl or presenting the cup for the Lampard Trust Handicap Chase or in the dirt yard of "her" clinic in Sylhet, surrounded by beaming doctors, and all with that look of fright. He wondered if even at the height of their influence, the Bolingbrokes had ever been quite so much in the eye. Jim was fed up with the district fawning on the Lampards and had hoped that Bolingbroke alone, with his ancient occupation of the place, might be an exception. Jim supposed it was the privilege of a gay man to penetrate the hearts of women and, like a doctor of the spirit, investigate their sad or splendid secrets. Jim felt disappointed that Jack had no more purpose in walking with him than to clear up a rural misunderstanding.

"Why should I?"

"There are some things I'm not able to tell you."

"I'm not inquisitive."

Bolingbroke shook his head in frustration. Jim detected a trace of lordliness in him, as if Jack were not used to saying something more than once. It passed across his nature like a cloud over a windy beach.

Jack said: "This has nothing to do with gossip. Promise me, Jim, that you won't think badly of me for keeping that picture."

"I promise." Jim's good temper was restored.

101

"My mother always liked Paradise Farm. She used to say we should never have left it."

"What? For Mount Royal?"

"Mount Royal House is a machine for destroying a family."

"I suppose it must be costly to run."

"I did not mean that." Once again, Jim detected the vestige of a patrician impatience. Jack said: "I meant: Once you decide you want people to stare at you, then you make room for all sorts of false notions." He touched Jim on the sleeve. "Don't be hard on Marina, Jim. Her parents were the most foolish people I ever met. Sometimes, Jim, I think spoiling is as bad as beating up. They did not look after her. She was not looked after."

"What do you mean? I don't understand."

"'Apart from the fact that they prostitute their daughters, the Lydian way of life is not unlike our own.'"

They stopped to let two young women, laughing and holding their hats and lop-sided from where their heels had pierced the turf, pass in a flash of colour.

"Do you know a gentleman by the name of Dark?"

Jim had turned and caught the ox eyes of one of the girls. With the greatest reluctance, he turned back and said: "I do."

"Do you have an opinion of him?"

"Yes. Unfavourable."

"He has written to me about Haze Common."

Jim halted while a farmer, recognised by his white trousers and white coat, chaffed with Bolingbroke. The man was a perfect square, his head flat, his shoulders broad and his legs short. At this rate, Jim thought, we will never make it to the barns. He had not grasped that Bolingbroke was not in a hurry, but on the contrary wished to spin out their passage arm-in-arm through the showground for as long as possible. Jack wished to show Brackshire, or at least the thirty thousand Brack Country men and women at the Royal Brightwell and West Show, that Jim was his friend. Jack judged, with the wisdom of five centuries in the district, that Brackshire would rather have Jim queer than foreign. All that passed Jim by. He had received little kindness in his life and was not attuned to recognise it.

"What's Haze Common to Mr Dark?" Jim asked, as they resumed. The topic did not much interest him.

"He is anxious that there is a shortage of affordable housing in Brackshire."

"Is there?" Jim was suspicious of good intentions in business.

"Well, Jim, on the one hand, if there were, you would see homeless people and tramps in the roads and lanes, as in my childhood. The people here are poor, by the standards of London and the counties around it, but they don't feel poor. They feel well off. If there were work here, there would be houses." He stopped. "Heavens, I'm the last person to ask. The fact is, Jim, my mother gave the Common to the village after the war."

"So that's that."

"Mr Dark disagrees. He says it has always been part of the Mount Royal estate, which belongs to Mr

Lampard. Mrs Dark, I believe, is a friend of Mr Lampard."

Jim, who really was something of a prig, was surprised that his friend stooped to gossip. He steered the conversation back to the point.

"Well, surely there is a record of your mother's gift?"

Jack did not answer. Jim thought that in order to answer, Jack would have to pass some comment or judgement on his mother's conduct or business practice, which he would not do. Jim thought: Perhaps in those days, a Bolingbroke's word was her bond. Jim rummaged in his mind for any social intelligence he needed.

"Jack, who or what is H.?"

Bolingbroke stopped walking. He said: "H., Jim, is H.R.H."

Jim was none the wiser.

"H., Jim, is the heir to the throne of Great Britain and Northern Ireland and some other countries, Jamaica, I think, and Canada and Australia. The Duke of Essex. A very estimable young man." He stopped dead. "Shall I present you? Do you wish to be presented, Jim?" He reached for Jim's arm and turned full about.

"No, thank you." Jim drew his arm away.

They passed a barn marked "Holstein", and another marked "Jersey".

"Comes for the rabbits."

"The rabbits?"

"Yes, Jim, the rabbits. Henry, Duke of Essex, likes shooting rabbits. It's very good here for rabbits. The sandy soil, you know?"

Jim could not understand why anybody who was not actually starving would want to shoot rabbits.

There was something incorrigible in Lord Bolingbroke. He said: "I believe the Duke of Essex likes it here for another reason: because it's not on the way anywhere, and he can pursue other interests away from the attentions of the photographers."

Jim had an inspiration. "Golf?"

A smile appeared on Lord Bolingbroke's sad face. "Yes, and some other things, as well."

They passed "Hereford", "British Limousin", "British Simmental", "South Devon"; and then "Any Other Beef or Dual-Purpose Breed". In this last, the men and women had a diligent, weathered, ragged air that fitted the bill. The children gave the impression that they had come into the world full grown.

"Ah," Jack said. "We're here."

Jim could not tell what impressions Bolingbroke took. Did he feel the heat from the animals, and the breath of cool air through the door, the sound of bellowing, the smell of onions and fried beef from the hamburger carts? Against the wall, tethered to a ring with a spotless white halter, and surrounded by a palisade of straw bales, was Bramble. Her coat was brushed, watered, chalked and painted, so that she looked not so much a cow as a sort of bovine prostitute. On her harness was a rosette marked "Reserve Champion". Of John there was no sign except his blue overall, hanging from a peg, and a milking cap.

"Do you want to sit down, Jack? There's a bale here."

"No, let me touch Bramble. I knew her dam and her dam's dam."

Jim took his hand and placed it on the cow's back, which shivered.

"What is it, my darling?"

Bramble turned her strumpet's eye on Jack.

"What is it?" He straightened. "Jim, I think she is in some discomfort. Would you look at her feet?"

That was more easily said then done. In coaxing up the feet, Jim brushed against an udder as hard as muscle. Jim said: "She's very full."

"They miss a milking to fool the judges. John Walker, in particular, does it to fool the judges. Would you very kindly find me a stool and pail?"

"That's all right, Jack. I can manage."

"Are you sure? And you'll get them both home?"

"Yes, I will."

"Thank you."

Jim accompanied his friend back to the Stewards' Enclosure and handed him over to an official in a bowler hat. Across from the barn was a milking station, but it was a suction system that Jim distrusted and Bramble had never had. Jim wondered if it would harm her, and anyway he would need to ask how to operate it. In all his life, Jim had never asked for help. He took off his jacket and wristwatch, washed his hands and put on John's overall and cap.

Jim thumped his head against the flank of the cow.

He felt a finger touch his back.

Irritated, he turned round and saw a woman, bent at the waist, smiling like sunshine. Erect at each side of her were two lean gentlemen-thugs in club or military ties. The woman straightened as if shot. Her left hand dropped to her skirt. Her face turned white as paper.

"Oh," she said. "I thought you were John Walker."

Jim stood up. He said: "I'm afraid he's not here."

Jim did not think he could say that John was in the beer-tent and was not fit for the company of women. He said: "His cow needed milking."

"Well, don't let us interrupt, old chap," said one of the gentlemen. He spoke with care and clarity, as if Jim were uneducated or half-witted. "Nice to see things done in the funny old way."

"I bet I know where old John is . . ." said the other man.

Jim was beneath notice. It was as if, in adopting the blue overall and cap to milk John Walker's cow, he had shed his personality and achievements and possessions. He was not the founder and first managing director of Finsoft or the farmer at Paradise Farm, but a mere clown. The woman had turned her back and was receding fast. In the dust and sunlight, she stumbled, and then recovered her poise. The men had to stride to keep up.

"Actually, Marina," one of the men was saying, "H. was asking why we continue to keep on the stock. It's only old Jack Bolingbroke and some of the other . . ." The rest was swallowed up in the dust and motes of light.

Jim had never been so angry. Mrs Lampard he left alone. Jim was not in the habit of judging women any more than he judged children. They stood outside his system of propriety. Where they did right, or where they did wrong, it was out of instincts that he could not comprehend and therefore could not share. What could he know of such a woman, insulated in her beauty and her money as if by cotton wool? To the men he swore a vengeance all the more terrible that it was not made precise. That one of the men, as Jim milled the tailings of his humiliation, was revealed as Tim Woodman, transformed from the boon companion of a fortnight before, blew Jim's anger into a fire. He would have set the whole showground in flames, sent animals, women and children shrieking in panic, the whole county dead and dying, and not felt any the better.

A more thoughtful man would have waited for his anger to subside, and recognised that he had gained something of value, for he now knew something of what it was to be John Walker. A more considerate man might have generalised the thought to this: that the poor, and the crippled, and the old-fashioned and hated and feared, the drunkard and the junkie and molester of children, the countryman and the clown are the privileged of society, for it is they who feel its movements on their backs and in their bellies and in their poor hearts. Jim was fortunate in that he was of only average mental discernment, and knew the sources of his anger no better than the sources of his contentment. The truth is that no man, least of all any man this side of thirty years of age, can bear to be of no account to a young woman. How much more so if that woman could not look at him, turned white and then red, scattered tears like dew, and ran out of the barn as fast as her town shoes would permit her; as fast, indeed, as if the very Furies were on her tail?

It helped not at all that Bramble would give no milk.

Jim swung the bucket out of the way. He caught Bramble's hoof on the back-swing.

"If you kick me, mistress, I swear to God I'll thump you."

It was no good. Caress or coax as he might, Bramble would not let down her milk. Jim went looking for John Walker. He combed the beer-tents and the barns and the carparks A to F. As he retraced his steps of the morning, the show became first familiar to him, then tedious, then hateful. Yet for some reason he could not fathom, he was in the best of moods. He thought, with the greatest pleasure: I used to own a business with ninety-two employees and annual revenues of £180,000,000, and here I am searching a provincial showground for a surly drunk. Deciding that some divinity precedes and guides the drunkard like the god that stands beside the Greek warrior in battle, Jim returned to the barn. Bramble was bellowing in pain.

The vet, whether out of idleness or to save Jim money, or perhaps indifferently, made up a syringe of oxytetracycline, lest the milk in the udder turn septic and set off a mastitis. Jim administered the injection, and coaxed Bramble into her trailer. As he picked his way along the avenues, he saw that though the Show was closed the showground was not empty, not at all. From the rear of the tent in the Stewards' Enclosure, a man and a woman burst out with their arms loaded with open champagne bottles. Someone else was dragging a plastic sack of what might have been *vols-au-vent*. Another had made a fire of fence slats, and amid the smoke and crackle of cheap lumber, a young girl was dancing. Something was familiar about her, but Jim could not recollect what it was. Sparks flew up in an arc and drifted with the smoke. Jim smelled roasting meat and petrol. It seemed that the Heir to the Throne of England and Jamaica and the Lady Lieutenant and His Honour the Mayor and the high sheriffs and the aldermen and the small television celebrities and the land agents and the dealers in four-wheel-drive vehicles had had their day. It was as if some other class or degree of person, neither noble nor merchant nor plebeian, but earth-dwelling and emerging only after dark, would now enjoy its Royal Show. To this class belonged Jim's employee John Walker. Jim realised, not for the first time, that he knew very little about Brackshire or indeed about anything.

All the while, he felt he had been struck between the shoulder blades, not by a knife or switchblade, but by a billionairess' finger.

CHAPTER
EIGHT

The Lost Commons

Jim rose early. He had slept for an hour, but woken with a bad conscience. It was not merely that he had promised Jack Bolingbroke to bring John Walker home and not done so, but that he always seemed to be doing Jack's bidding, as if he were a vassal in a timeless and God-appointed system of subordination. He fetched Argos from his kennel and set off through the dew to Haze Common.

John Walker's cottage was not hard to find. Amid the pensioners' privet and honeysuckle, here was a house with steel window frames, an old hand-pump by the kitchen door and valerian growing out of holed tin buckets. On the roof, which was a little crazy, the letter B had been picked out in mathematical tiles. Jim wondered if this was the very last of Jack's estate cottages, where once a man had lived and worked his harvest and in the mean times fed a cow on bad grass or turned over an acre of arable land. Jim felt, just as he had felt at the Show, that he was out at the end of a bough which would not much longer bear his weight.

Pressing open the door, Jim came into a cold kitchen. On the stone floor were newspapers, tin dog bowls and a big cardboard box, and in it chicks squeaking under a heat lamp. On the window ledges were old bottles of veterinary medicine or alcohol. As his eyes became accustomed to the dawn through the dirty steel window frames, Jim saw a cold grate and beside it a greasy armchair with a figure in it, legs extended. It was John Walker in a fitful sleep. Jim turned to go, and then thought that he should make a better examination. He had heard of drunks choking to death or drowning in vomit.

John was lying with his face to the ceiling. His breathing was not regular, but like the waves on a beach, each breath longer than the one before, and then a spasm or snore, and then the process repeated. In his right hand was the cold stub of a roll-up cigarette. From the scorches on the arm of the chair, Jim could see that it had been some years since John Walker had bothered to climb up to his bed. His left hand was closed on something white. The whiteness absorbed the morning light and did not pay it back. It was not marble or paper, but something lustreless and matte and granular like pipe clay. From under his little finger, there protuded about an inch of white which looked like a woman's leg smashed at the shin. From under the thumb, there was a shapely neck, missing the head.

This same tired light was elsewhere in the room: for example, above the chick nursery, the stove, a copy of *Native Breeds of Cattle of Great Britain* and an open drawer to an old pine kitchen table. From a distance, Jim saw into the drawer. On a layer of cotton wool that filled the base of the drawer were little figures of women or rather parts of women: a pair of buttocks and hips, a pretty forearm, a bosom covered in drapery, a head of hair and eyes under a diadem. Even Jim, who was no kind of scholar, could see they were very old. Describe what you see, not what you don't know, you idiot! The cotton wool had faded to a nicotine yellow. It appeared to Jim that at least one and perhaps many of the figurines had been laid there many years before. These model women were what kept John in the district. They were John's profession. They were the reasons for the trench or hole in the ground that had almost broken Jim's leg on his night walk, and for that fear or unease he felt at night but Argos did not. A voice in his head repeated the same sentence or small variations of it over and over and over again: "Why should the dog bark, if he hears his friend?"

Why on earth would Argos bark at the man who had bred him?

Jim turned and said, so low as to be beneath a whisper: "Enough of your night-digging, John Walker."

Coming out onto the Common, Jim saw four men driving in posts from which barbed wire hung limply, as on a toy battlefield. Following them was a one-and-a-half ton truck, with dozens of round larch posts propped up against the gantry.

"What the hell are you doing?"

The men took no notice. Jim placed himself in the way of one of them. The man slid past him to the van, eyes averted. He had an old-fashioned look and bad teeth. Jim looked round. The pensioners had retreated behind their curtains.

"This is common land. You cannot fence it."

The man attempted to get past him. "Excuse me," the man said.

Jim lost his patience. "You are breaking the law. Who told you to do this?"

He mumbled something.

"Who?"

"McCain."

"What the hell has it to do with Gordon McCain?"

Argos growled.

"Good doggy . . ."

Jim spun round into the luminescent jacket of a police officer. Behind him a police cruiser and another officer idled. Jim suspected that a police vehicle had never before passed down The Street in Haze Common in all recorded time. Beyond it, parked by the duck pond, was the purple school bus of the travelling couple.

"Ah, officer. Thank you for coming. These gentlemen are restricting access to common land, which is an offence."

"Are you a resident here, sir?"

"I live at Paradise Farm."

"Is that in Haze Common?"

"It's down that lane you see there."

"So you don't have rights on the Common."

"No, but the village people do."

"Well, then, if you don't mind moving on."

A sort of residue of Jim's anger of the day before flared back to life.

"They're breaking the law, officer."

114

"As I understand it, there is some dispute about the ownership of the Common. We're here to prevent an incident."

"Ownership has nothing to do with it. The common rights coexist with the owner's rights. That's the whole point of common land."

Jim's sentence, with its fancy distinctions, disintegrated against the luminescent jacket.

"We're here to keep the peace."

"Damn the peace. What matters is justice."

The police officer looked evil. Jim had gone too far. He had trespassed on to the monopoly of force in Great Britain. For an instant, he saw an infinity of iron corridors and uniformed men with a taste for order and regulations. He strode off.

At the end of the Common, just at the point where it funnelled out into the fields, stood a garage. Jim had once brought his trailer to have its lights fixed. There was an old building open to the Common which might once have been the smithy and was now the garage office, a couple of diesel pumps, a workshop with a pitched roof of asbestos tiles and, before it, a lumber of vehicles whose wheels Argos inspected with care. The darkness of the workshop made Jim dizzy. There was a stench of vulcanised rubber. On the oily floor, his footsteps made no sound. He might have been barefoot on a silk carpet.

Out of the gloom, he saw two vehicles raised on hydraulic jacks and three men and a woman seated on decayed car seats, drinking hot tea from mugs. They were as sunburnt as Arabs encamped under the pylons of Thebes. They looked at Jim without interest or kindness. Argos halted with one paw raised.

Jim thought: I have chosen to be on my own. I have no corporation at my back, no lawyers, no secretary, no expense codes, no security detail. I have chosen to do my own dirty work. He said: "I'm Jim Smith from Paradise Farm. Which of you gentlemen is Mr Cedric Medley?"

Two young men, alike as Romany peas, nodded at an older man. The lady, who may have been their mother, rose with a flourish and bore her mug of tea aloft and away.

Jim pressed on. "We need . . ." He began again. "The police are useless. The wire must be taken down tonight. If it's up tomorrow, it stays up and that's the end of your Common."

One of the boys spoke, but not to Jim. "Herbert would," he said.

"He's daft."

"And John Walker, when he wakes himself."

Mr Medley hished.

"There's Harold. He's on days now."

Jim understood that he had broken in on a discussion of precisely the matter at issue. It was not a discussion such as he had attempted with the police officer, but of a wholly different composition and one that did not require much speech. Jim wondered why all these people went by the Christian names of seventy years ago.

Mr Medley spoke. "What's it to Paradise Farm?"

It was the question the police officer had posed. Jim was at a loss. What was it to him? Did it indeed matter to him if concrete was poured the length of the Common? None of these people had animals to graze, except the boys with their horses. Did he secretly want the country kept as it was, frozen at the moment of his arrival and inert and changeless until his death? Did not all the world have an owner? Was there any ground without its lord?

"Nothing," said Jim. "What's it to you, Mr Medley?"

To say the boys smirked would be exaggeration. What is true is that nobody before Jim had ever, in their hearing, spoken thus to their father, who burst out: "If Jack Bolingbroke had been in the spill, this wouldn't have happened!"

That went over Jim's head. He said: "Shall we meet at Paradise Farm?"

The boys fell into frowns.

"You just leave it with us," said Mr Medley. That tyrant, that horse-Caesar and grease-Napoleon, put his tea down on the hub of an alloy wheel.

Jim was disappointed to be no part of the adventure. He said: "No firearms, please."

The boys burst out laughing. Oh, how they laughed! Jim called Argos, turned and padded out. As he passed down the lane, he said: "Well, they'll remember something about me when the waters have closed above my head. They'll remember me for saying: 'No firearms, please.'"

In that, Jim was correct. His appearance at the Shire Garage decided the outcome of the family discussion and the fate of Haze Common in the twentieth century. Mrs Medley had been for action, and Willie and Walter, the boys, were as always with her. Cedric Medley, whose family had been the blacksmiths at Haze Common since Waterloo, shoeing horses and mending thresher belts and forging crankshafts whenever the rain came down, was neither opposed to change nor inclined to make an enemy of McCain, or whoever stood behind McCain. The Robinsons (they all knew) were lubberly and feckless sods, the wire so slack and the posts just a foot driven in, you could blow them over with a fag in your mouth and a missed gear with the rolling machines would do the rest. Yet the possibility that the Londoner might do something, might call in men from Brightwell or who knows where, was not only intolerable in itself but might have consequences for the balance of forces in Haze Common. So that was that.

Jim followed events in the *Brightwell Advertiser*. Two officers, despatched from Brightwell to reassure the villagers and prevent an incident, were absent from the Common for a short period each side of 11 p.m. By the time they returned, over the whole western end of the Common the posts had been laid flat and the wire cut into one-and-a-half-metre lengths. At the eastern end, they found private security contractors working for Lampard Estates in altercation with villagers. Mrs Jane Williamson, of 2, The Street, returning from bowls, had been frightened by the security contractors' Alsatian dogs and been unable to enter her cottage. She had called to her neighbours for help. No arrests were made, though Mr John Walker, of Bolingbroke Cottage, The Street, was cautioned for threatening behaviour. Once the crowd disbanded, the officers made a tour of inspection and saw that the eastern end of the fencing had also been laid flat. Mr Richard Dark, solicitor for Lampard Estates, said that the estate had received intelligence of plans to establish a travellers' encampment on its property and had acted decisively. He complained at the reckless abuse of estate property and said that it would seek criminal damages against the Commons Committee and Mr Walker. Mrs Eileen Medley, chair of the parish council and co-proprietor of the Shire Garage at the eastern end of the Common, had volunteered to store the posts and wire securely until the matter of ownership could be resolved in the courts. The Commons Committee had retained the services of Pinch and Keepit of Brightwell, and would be holding a programme of fundraising events, including trotting races and cream teas, over the summer.

Two things the newspaper did not say, but occurred to Jim. If the posts were laid down just in those few minutes when the police officers were ordering at McDonald's in Brightwell, there must have been more young men at work that evening than Willie and Walter Medley, many more. Perhaps the Brack Country was not so empty of men as Jim had thought. The second point was more perplexing. The operation to fence Haze Common, from the strands of limp wire to the two dazed hippies that were its pretext, was haphazard and slipshod in its execution.

119

Jim lacked both imagination and social experience. He did remember what Jack Bolingbroke had said about Lampard and Emilia Dark at the showground. He recognised that he had been unfair to his friend and what he had thought mere vulgar gossip might be a true change in affairs that would affect all of them. If Lampard, weary of his terrified princess, had indeed fallen under Mrs Dark's spell, then fortunate Mr Dark, who now enjoyed ascendancy over the richest man in the Brack Country. Or was it that Lampard craved a town at his park gates? Did Charles Lampard need money?

And all the while, Jim thought: What are those *things* that John Walker digs out of my fields?

CHAPTER
NINE

Sea Bathing at Brightwell

The house rose like a mountain from his dream. Jim had never seen a house so large and square, with so many tall windows flashing back the sun, and a pediment like that of the Parthenon. A path had been mowed to the base of a flight of stone stairs. They climbed them, Jean resting her hand on the stone urn at the top. Here was a terrace, all long grass and moths, and the mown path carrying on to a double door of glass panes. Beyond it was the thump of a record player. Jeanie seemed to relax. In front of the door was a very tall man with long hair and sunglasses, turning round slowly and scratching his head, as if he had dropped something on the ground. He had on a beautiful pink shirt that hugged his skinny chest and jeans patched and slashed with velvet at the base. He had in his hand a cigarette which had gone out. He was barefoot.

"Halloo." Jean waved her hand before his face.

"Groovy hat," he said, and then recognised her. His face broke into the sweetest smile. "Groovy hat," he said again.

"I brought Jim."

The man turned and some of the brightness spilled on Jim. "Hi," he said.

"Jim's staying."

"Good," he said, and turned away in shyness.

Jim was baffled. The dream did not seem quite right. Where were the footmen that went with this palace, the gardeners weeding the scalding alleys, the nurses pushing their perambulators? Where were the labourers who came out of the war in bits? The music boomed.

"He's at school, Jack."

"Poor boy. I was sacked, you know. From Westchester College. For queering."

"Everybody knows that," said Jean.

"He didn't. You didn't, did you, man?"

"No, sir."

"Come in," he said. "You must be thirsty."

Jim could see the man really liked Jean, even though he said he was queer. They stepped towards the blinding panes and the rumble of music. Jim lost his nerve. Jean was going to go off with her friends, and he had not brought anything to read.

"Buck up, you," she said at the doors. The sun wheeled round in the door panes and blinded him. As he stepped through, she took his right hand, and swung it in hers as they clattered over a marble floor towards the music. "Jack, is that it?" she said.

"Is that what?"

"*Leaves of Fire.*"

"Yep. Markie brought it up. We played it all night. Far-arsing-out."

"Watch your fucking language, Lord Bolingbroke."

They came into the bellowing room. Though there was furniture in it, people were sitting on the floor. Or rather, spread across a worn Persian carpet were cushions, an ashtray and a large map held down in the corner by books and a long ruler. In one of the window bays, haloed by sunshine, a graceful boy was rolling a cigarette on a record cover.

Jean lunged for the record sleeve.

"Bug off, you bloody fish," said the boy, raising sleeve, papers and tobacco above his head.

"Mark, this is Jim. He's staying with me."

His angel face turned ugly.

"Jim's at school."

"Why do you want to be there, man? Why do you want to waste your life at some school?" He raised his cigarette to his lips, and Jean snatched the record sleeve.

"You cunt," he said.

Jean slid to the floor. The record sleeve showed her bare-breasted in an old tree in a meadow. She looked closely at herself and then, as if satisfied, tossed the sleeve on the floor. Jim, who had never seen a naked girl, tried not to look at it.

"Here's some lemonade, man." Lord Bolingbroke stood above them, holding a tray with a jug, a silver bucket of ice and mismatched glasses.

"Here's some lemonade, man," said Markie, imitating his Brackshire voice.

"Just lemonade, Jack?"

"Just lemonade, Jack," said Markie, imitating Jean's voice.

Jim did not know what libertine game they were playing. He did not know if Jean would look after him or go off with her friends. He wished they were back at her house, or in the car in the lanes, or outside with the prancing dog.

"Can you handle it?" Lord Bolingbroke was by the record-player, the arm in his fingers. He still had his sunglasses on.

"Mmm," said Jean.

She put her head in her hands. Jim did the same, till he felt a light tap on the shoulder. Mark was holding out the cigarette. He meant Jim to take it. Jim took it.

"That'll turn them on at St Perve's."

He didn't know what to do. Without looking up, Jean took the cigarette, took a deep breath, then shut her mouth and turned to Jim, with a severe look.

"Open wide," she said.

Jim opened his mouth to speak and felt the warmth of her face and then the touch of her lips on his. Sweet smoke engulfed his face and eyes.

"My oh my," said Mark.

"If Her Ladyships is quite ready," said Lord Bolingbroke.

The music sounded as if it had fallen from heaven.

> He wanted twenty-two womens
> Out of the Hampton Hotel

124

And all the while Jim's mind went round and round: I've met a hippie, and smoked a cigarette . . .

"Why's he so scared? What's to be scared of?"

"Markie, please."

"Just shut up, damn you, Mark." Jean was spitting fire across Jim.

"Oh God," said Lord Bolingbroke. He looked at Jim in agony. Jim's eyes were damp, so he got up and went out into the sunshine. He wanted to get away from human beings. There was no shade, just stone and grass and moths, and the dog circling and receding every time he stepped towards her. Jim had met a hippie, and smoked a cigarette, and kissed a girl . . . If only these things had happened on separate days, for he could not sustain himself under such a rain of novelty. He went down off the terrace, and on down the mown path to a dry basin, with a sea god baring a green and brown chest where water had once spilled from a fountain. The basin was littered with pine needles and broken bamboos. He had met a homosexual, and smoked a reefer, and heard *Leaves of Fire*, and kissed a woman . . . At the end of the path was a pavilion made of shells and, beyond it, the cooler green of fields and reeds. Maybe there was a pond or a lake. The dog stood before the pavilion as if on a long, long tether. Inside, it was dark and dank. Jean was sitting on a stone bench, her bare legs drawn up beneath her. She said: "Do you want to sit with me?"

"Do *you* think I should not go back to school, Jean?"

Her eyes widened. "Don't bother about Markie. He's out of his head."

"Why?"

"Windowpane."

The word made Jim sit down. "What's windowpane?"

"I'll tell you on Sunday." She took his hand. "Jack really likes you. He said he'd kill me if I hurt a hair on your head."

"I'll kill him."

"My, you've turned fierce. What happened to the boy who couldn't say boo to a goose!" She stood up. "Come on, let's swim."

"Oh no."

"Let's go."

"I haven't . . ."

"Don't be such a stiff. Anywhere, there's nobody around except those hippies."

"Please, Jean."

Jim's eyes were wet again, but she had gone. Jim saw her in the sunlight, the dog making tunnels through the long grass. At the edge of the lake was a place muddy with footprints.

"Close eyes."

He shut his eyes till he heard a splash. Her dress was on the ground. She was swimming out into the lake like an athlete. Jim took off his shoes and socks, and his shirt, and his jeans. The water was cold, and the bottom slimy, so he struck out, startled by a moorhen. Jean was treading water under a big sky.

"Windowpane is L.S.D., Jim. The best of the best. From where your girlfriend comes from."

She dived and Jim dived after her. He followed the gleam of her knickers and breast in the gloom. He must let everything go and start again. I must follow this gleaming which is the only thing worth anything in this world below . . .

"Turn around," she cried. "I'm getting out."

. . . and oh, if only the world could stop so he could count the things that had happened today. He'd kissed a girl, and swum without his clothes . . .

Jeanie held out his clothes as he slid and scampered on the mud. She looked different with her hair wet, but still pretty. "Come on, let's just go. Those freaks have forgotten us. What the fuck!"

Jim looked up. He could see a tractor on the slope, and a man in overalls peeling back the engine cover.

"I knew it. That fucking peep."

"I think he's broken down."

"Like fuck he has. Fucking John Walker, you're going to regret this."

In the kitchen at Paradise Farm, Jeanie fell quiet. "Have you had fun, Jim?"

"Yes. I mean, I don't know."

She shook herself as if making some resolution, and turned to go out.

"Where are you going?"

"Come if you want."

He followed her through the long rooms. Posters, lamps, desks, rugs concertinaed into one another. Jim bade farewell to them, for he did not expect to see them again, not in this world. When he saw them again, it would be as another man. They climbed the stairs. Jim forgot to breathe. Jean opened the door into a bedroom flooded with afternoon light. It smelled of dried tobacco and wilting roses. A voice began to speak in his troubled head. It spoke in Greek. If you sleep with a goddess in dreams, that signifies your death, for it is a prevision of the congress the soul has with the gods, which happens as soon as the soul leaves the body in which it dwells. For the same reason, if the dream is of a person of great size, that is death. For the same reason, if your dream is of a person of unnatural beauty, that is also your death.

A path had been mowed to the base of a flight of stone stairs. Jim climbed up the broken steps and rested his hand on the stone urn at the top. Here was a terrace, all long grass and moths, and the mown path. Moths blew against a double door of panes. In his dream, he had heard a record player and his first sight of Jack was of a tall man with long hair and sunglasses, turning round on bare feet and scratching his head, as if he had dropped something on the ground. Jim signalled to Argos to wait and pushed at the door. The sun wheeled round in the door panes and blinded man and dog.

As he adjusted his eyes to the hall light, he saw Jack Bolingbroke seated in an upright chair. It occurred to Jim that his friend had shed all attachments. House and park in their ruin no longer embodied his personality. He sat on a chair because he was not strong enough to stand. He turned towards the sun and said: "Is that you, Jim?"

"Yes. How are you, Jack?"

"I am neither well nor ill, Jim, have sometimes strange feelings about me, cold streams running over my shoulders and down my back, and restless nights. Do you want some wine?"

Jim shook his head and then remembered Jack could not see him. He looked up at Jean Lampard's portrait. He expected to see it altered on a second viewing, as if to accommodate his tumultuous dreams. What he had not expected was its beauty. It was as if, that first time he came, he had not the faculty or wherewithal to respond to beauty. The picture was beautiful not just because a woman's body is to a man the incorporation of happiness, of which beauty is the counterpart in the world of vision, but because of some hint or breath of permanence. The hat she wore was not, Jim saw, purely an erotic accessory. If Mark Neal intended it as a mere vulgar device to show that the rest of her was naked (like a garter belt or tattoo on a pole dancer), the passage of the years had transformed that intention. Old-fashioned, even quaint, the hat was a vestige of the 1960s to remind the viewer that the body was otherwise eternal. Jim saw, for the first time, why the picture had in such a short time become so valuable in money.

"No, thank you, Jack. I brought some cigarettes. I'll light one for you."

Bolingbroke smiled. "Cigarettes can shorten your life," he said.

Jim put the lighted cigarette in the corner of Jack's mouth.

"How did you know I liked to smoke?"

He said: "I saw you as a young man in my dream."

129

This statement, which had cost Jim so much, Jack took as polite conversation. He drew on the cigarette and said: "For reasons only a woman would understand, Jeanie married Charles Lampard and came up to your house, to Paradise Farm. I think it was just a weekend place, at first. This must have been 1967. Lampard's father had been an ordinary crook in Brightwell who had done well out of the Americans in the war. The son went up to London and made money in, I think, the motor trade in the Goldhawk Road. Jeanie rode over here one day, bareback, in just a summer dress and flip-flops and the hat in Markie's picture, and that dog of hers, how could anybody resist her? In those days, you know, Jim, her face was everywhere. I thought, when I saw her dismount, it's all over with the past, thank God, we can start again."

"What breed of dog?"

"A saluki."

"Didn't you ask where she came from?"

"Jim, you must understand that in those days you didn't ask such things. The whole point was that origins had been abolished. Markie's people were Jehovah's Witnesses in Cheswold, and yet we became friends. That was the great appeal of the movement, especially to people like me."

Bolingbroke came down to earth. He said: "We made a pact, Jeanie and I."

"Why didn't you keep to it, damn you!"

"Don't you be damning anybody, Jim Smith."

It was as if a blindfold had been lifted from Jim's eyes, and he saw, for an instant of an instant, into the mystery of existence. He saw that his friend's condition, as he sat there, blind, dejected, amid the ruins of his inheritance and the deaths of his friends, was not his own fault or a set of accidents or the effect of history or taxation or constitutional reform or a mere social revolution, but the work of a single unforgiving spirit. Jim's heart went out to meet him, but, before it had taken a step, as it were, it turned back on itself. Could it be that his humiliation in business, his dead lambs and dried-up cows were premonitions of the same destiny?

Jack spoke: "We agreed if either of us died we would come back to Brightwell Links, at the place by the coastguard station where we used to launch the boat, on her birthday. It was Jeanie's idea."

"And you never went."

"The twenty-third of July came round the first year, and I was too scared to go, and then I began to have trouble seeing."

"What if I came with you this time? I'll be your eyes for you."

"No."

"Why the hell not, Jack? She needs you to do something for her, there, wherever she is."

"No."

"Yes, Jack."

Jack whispered: "The world is not what it was. It is growing old and decrepit. What goodness there was is going out of it. I think as the old order breaks down, all manner of strange appearances will become commonplace." He stopped. There seemed no point proceeding on these high matters. He said: "You know what she wants, don't you?"

"She comes to me in my dreams, Jack."

" 'In a robe brighter than firelight, her head brushing the rafters.' "

"Yes."

Jack said: "Jim, they're not like us. They can be kind to people they like, but they are implacable. They are not like human beings."

"Oh, on the contrary, they're all too like us. That's the problem."

"Don't go to the Links, Jim. Swear to me you won't go."

"I will not swear. I will go."

"If you go, I will not see you again, and that will break my heart."

"I will go."

Jim turned to leave, then had an idea. "What happened to the dog, Jack?"

"Not found, either. Do not go, Jim."

Jim stumbled out on to the scalding terrace. The sight of Argos' head, rigid with alarm, brought him to earth. He patted the animal's flank. The dog looked at him as if to say: Whatever it is, I will help with it.

On 23 July Jim set off with Argos to Brightwell Links. To himself, he was just going for a walk, and naturally took his dog with him. He wrapped his gun in polythene against the sea air and put it in his coat. A notice told him dogs must be on leads, to keep them away from the nesting terns, and so for the first time he put a lead on Argos. He soon took it off.

Across the marshes, the wind was bending the sedge grass and turning the leaves of the alders silver. Flocks of grey geese were grazing down the turf. Clouds flooded the upper air. Silver sails passed to and fro amid the fields as if sea and land had changed places. Jim followed the sea wall where it separated the fields from the saltings to a point where he could see the old coastguard station upside down in the air. From the Ordnance Survey map, the station was four miles away, but in the haze it might have been at Cape Hatteras. High tide was not until eight that evening, but there was no purpose in dawdling.

The path through the saltings was slippery from the tide. Every few yards, Jim had to spring over a gut or channel. At one such crossing, the far bank was steep and his boots slipped and were soaked. He decided to take them off and walk barefoot where the samphire held the ground a little tighter. Pairs of oystercatchers circled him, squeaking in panic or anger. The coastguard station resolved itself into a square building of red brick.

Jim shared his sandwich with Argos.

It was as if the air had been rinsed. Tints of light caught the rims of black pools, shells, thrift. In a sort of exhilaration, Jim quickened his step. Looking back, he saw miles and miles of marsh and, hanging in the air, the church towers of who knew where. He also saw that Argos was halted. Beyond him, the tide was racing in like a river in spate. Turning again, Jim saw the coastguard station had sunk into a mirror. There was a sea on both sides of them. Jim did not know what to do, but knew that whatever he did, he must do it now. Argos raced up and down the water's edge, started, barked, prepared to spring in, lost heart, went back to his running.

"Stop that! Sit!"

Jim clipped on the lead and then sprang in. The water made nothing of man and dog. As he went beneath the surface, he felt himself pulling Argos down by the neck. His eyes opened on vortexes of sand. He thought: I'll have to let Argos go or he'll drown from my weight. He surfaced and saw the dog paddling. He drew Argos close and got a claw across his face for his pains. He struck out across the stream towards the land, but made no headway. He saw Brightwell Light, poking through the woods and thought: Let's run with the stream, that way Argos can keep his head above water, and we might hit something on the way.

"Stop paddling, lad. Just float. Keep your strength."

As Jim settled himself, Argos began to drag. Jim thought: He has no stamina, but as he weakens, he is less likely to injure himself. As they raced down the tide, he kept the lighthouse in sight. Every so often, he put his foot down into the void below.

"It's all right, we'll be dropped in the end."

Jim was thinking: At some point, I'll have to let go. I will not give my life for Argos, any more than he will give his life for me. The other thought was this: Jack warned me not to go. Is this what she wanted to do to Jack all those years ago? What does she want?

134

If a person, like a cat, has nine lives, Jim had used one of them. He was eighteen again and lying in the Bab al-Hawa cemetery, off Saadoun Street in Baghdad, which was nothing if not convenient, for he was dying. Though he did not know it, a young man had blown up a Nissan truck stocked with 500lbs of hexagene outside the old Iraqi Airways office, and the blast had thrown him into the cemetery. After a while, he began to feel cold and then to shake. His teeth clashed and chattered. He had no control of his hands or his feet or his mouth and voice. He thought he must shake himself to death. Though he did not know it, a portion of the engine casing of the truck had embedded itself in his back and he was dying of shock. Across the blue sky overhead aircraft passed to and fro, puffing out metal chaff to divert the ground artillery. The chaff sparkled like the wings of doves in a mosque courtyard. Jim thought: By the time that metal falls down to earth, I shall be dead.

Jim opened his eyes on an expanse of white sea. For some reason, Argos' face and mouth were rimmed with salt and vomit. Around them both were snapping black flags. Jim's teeth were chattering so much he thought he must shake himself to pieces. Ahead was a iron buoy and a bell on an iron tower that tolled as it swung in the water. So this, thought Jim, is the famous Gate of Air through which all mortal creatures must pass. His arms were being dragged down by a dead weight. He could hold on no longer. He let go.

Through the tumbled grave monuments, a small man in military uniform waddled towards Jim. From somewhere was the sound of a bell, and a barking dog, which was strange in Iraq for, as everybody knows, the Prophet abominated both bells and dogs. Behind the man were two medical orderlies wearing white coats splashed with blood and tissue and dragging semi-automatic rifles. The man's face filled the sky.

"Are you still with us, dear friend?" The man's courage was infectious.

"I was on my way."

"Shall I try to bring you back?"

"Why not?"

"Why not, indeed?"

Argos was swimming towards the ringing buoy. Jim held onto his tail.

CHAPTER
TEN

England from the Air

August stumped in. Coming to the Brightwell road, Jim found it a procession of inexplicable traffic. In the lanes were open-topped cars and young men in sunglasses. At home, the telephone ceased to ring. The post brought only circulars, or a charity invitation from the Lampards with a girlish *Please Come!* scribbled on it. Jim, who disapproved of charity, threw it in the bin beneath the kitchen sink. He gave up checking his email. It was as if the machines that set people in motion, whirring them round and round, were disabled or stood idle. Jim felt the whole of England had joined him in his condition of idleness. He felt as he imagined a drunkard feels on Christmas Eve.

John Walker took his holiday. There seemed at first no change to his habits or occupations. He came each day to Paradise Farm, tended the stock and the kitchen garden, mended gutters and fences. John's holiday seemed to consist only in that he ceased to speak to his employer. He did not answer Jim's greeting at noon or bid him goodbye in the evening. Well, Jim thought, there'll be time enough to interrogate him and, meanwhile, he will have a good rest.

Nature was in a trance. Through thick trees, scorched hayfields receded into infinity. Far away in the fields, there was the flash of a windscreen. In the dusk, a deluded haze settled on Paradise Farm, in which time seemed to be extinguished, and nothing moved but wood pigeons, clapping their wings like wooden shutters in a gale or tumbling like stones in the leaden air. In the heat, Jim caught cold, and lay out among the raspberry canes in the fruit cage. Nature fell apart, like a clod of earth held only by strings of root. Every now and then, he reached out for fruit to soothe his thirst and fever.

Argos lay for hours on end on his side on the gravel. Jim suspected that his dog had gone to the limit of his strength, and beyond, and would need many weeks to recoup it. The walk to the pasture exhausted him. That day in the Bristol Channel, at the cost of great suffering and injury, that would mark him all his short life, Argos had achieved something that he would not forget. Jim thought: If there is such a thing as happiness among dogs, Argos is happy.

Jim knew he should call on Jack, but what would he say? That Jack was right, and he had escaped drowning only through the courage and fidelity of his dog? Jim could not tolerate this perplexity. He would find the answer, which he felt was not abstruse or distant but near at hand, a little bit to this side or to that side, just the fraction of a step. Then he would see his friend.

For the first time since his brief schooldays, Jim began to read. At the second-hand bookseller in Brightwell, he bought a broken copy of the Rev.

Astley's *Antiquities of Brackshire*, as well as *Great Farmers of the West* and his own copy of *Native Breeds of Cattle of Great Britain*. The impressions Jim had formed of Brackshire, the knowledge that had stuck to him on his walks by day and night, like burrs on a jacket, was here presented as history. Jim recognised that he might have saved himself a great deal of trouble. Always bloody re-inventing the wheel!

In the Middle Ages, Brightwell had been the first port of the west, bringing in corn and linen, sending out wool from sheep grazed on the flat meadows behind the town. Children and young men were put to weaving cloth. Churches sprung up like orchids in a meadow. On the eve of the Black Death, the country was the richest in all England.

The land was so good that it yielded more than was needed to feed and clothe the man who worked it, who therefore married, and his wife brought up children who, not being required on the good land, were set to weaving or making shoes or harness, the surplus of which brought in money, which built the churches and the first brick or flint farms. Then, in the reign of Henry VIII, Brightwell Abbey was pulled apart. Lawyers and attorneys such as Francis Boling made themselves estates, running fold-courses of sheep through the devastated villages, overstocking the commons, driving the people onto Brightwell Heath and the Badsands, where they merged with the tinkers and Egyptians, and fought with three rabbits for two blades of grass. Jim thought it was rather like Russia after the fall of the Soviet Union, in which years of

139

accumulated capital came tumbling into the laps of new men such as Boling, and enough to see them through to the present. For was not Jack Bolingbroke as much a monument of Brackshire as a church or a place name or a piece of old river pasture?

Elevated to the nobility, the Bolingbrokes took the wrong side in the war between King and Parliament and, at the Revolution of 1688, went briefly into exile. On 20 October, 1719, in the presence of four witnesses at Jenkinson's Coffee House in the Strand, London, the third Earl of Bolingbroke sold the banker Thomas Beasley £100,000 nominal of East India Company stock short for delivery by 25 August, 1721 for £250,000. East India was then trading at £360 per £100 nominal. When the South Sea Bubble burst, and with it the prices of all joint-stock securities, Bolingbroke was able to buy the promised stock in a single transaction at less than par. His profit, according to Beasley's testimony to the House of Commons, was £372, 762 10/-, the income of which alone was enough to build and furnish Mount Royal House, or the "Bear Pit", as the London wits called it. The capital Bolingbroke employed to endow his daughters — all married dukes, to marl thirty thousand acres of the Badsands, and to introduce the new-fangled four-course crop rotation that he had studied during his Jacobite exile in the Low Countries. The best farm tenants came from all over England and Scotland, bringing with them new breeds of cow and sheep and pig. The Brightwell and West Agricultural Assocation became, for a period of about a generation, a hotbed of scientific husbandry.

The prosperity was short-lived. The cloth trade migrated to Yorkshire, where there was coal to power the looms and spinning machinery, and the water was better. The people wandered away. The Bolingbrokes fell into a life of cold mutton, backgammon, netting pike in The Maiden, small accidents, cribbage, pregnant maidservants, rhubarb, smallpox and blancmange. There was no coal to be mined, or alum, no daffodils to entrance romantic tourists, no castles, hills, clans, heather and imprisoned queens, no sea bathing. Fearful that they might raise the wages of farm labour, the fifth Earl kept out the railways. The harbour at Brightwell silted up, and the town found itself stranded behind riptides — where a child was lost every second year — or interminable saltmarsh haunted by wildfowlers and the Royal Society for the Protection of Birds. The Bolingbrokes won a Victoria Cross in the Great War and lost four sons. The land would have gone back to heath but for the men — Irwin, Britain, McCain — who came down from the West Riding in 1919 and bought the Bolingbroke farms for nothing. Too important to serve in World War II, these men ploughed up the village greens, laid runways for the United States Air Force and pilfered their machines. The demobbed countrymen found American tractors in their cottages.

Those were bonanza years. Each night, the farmers said to themselves: This will not last. We will go back to living in our boots in our kitchens. Is that so easy when you have taken to hounds and champagne; or, like

141

Mike and Julian Britain, played a four-ball at Hangman's Lane, St Kitts, with Sir Leroy Nurse and Sir Viv Phipps; or, like Bill Irwin, handed Verena van der Zee over a stile and taken a left and right off her magnificent chest? Even their prejudice against education dissolved when the Irwin girl won a scholarship to Cambridge. Good-hearted and also shy, they could not bear to see the men they had laid off, never stirred from their vehicles, sent their sons and daughters to boarding schools, instructed their wives to shop in Brightwell or even Chipstable. Holidays they took ever further abroad. Too solitary and suspicious to co-operate, they bid the price of the Badsands ever higher and higher and blamed Lampard and Jim.

"May I have this?" Jim had, for the second time in his life, entered a bookshop. The proprietor, to whom he felt unwelcome, took the book and looked for his marks on the inside front cover.

"Not in E.S.T.C.," he grumbled. "Brightwell printing. Scarce title. Two hundred pounds."

Jim sensed that to this man the verb was as hateful an item as soap or toothpaste or a customer. As he came out of the bookshop, Jim saw Harriet Woodman climbing into a four-wheel-drive vehicle.

"Harriet!"

She glared at him. Jim saw that to have accosted Harriet Woodman in the Brightwell High Street in August was not quite honourable, as if he had come on her in her nightgown or having laddered a stocking or broken a shoe heel. Jim wondered if there were something disgraceful in her shopping, a microwaveable meat pie, perhaps, or chain-store underlinen. Or was it that, in this plebeian setting, Harriet Woodman could not assume her complete social form? Like an angel in the depths, she struggled to stay down. Or was it — and here Jim lost his footing — the season of the year, this dead, hot August, where to be in Brackshire was to be so out of fashion as to risk social retribution? She should be on some cool Scots moor, dressed in a tailored coat and skirt, cracking with fund managers and shooting red grouse in the lungs.

They kissed without warmth.

"How's business, Harriet?"

About to close the driver's door on him, Harriet halted. Now business, Jim thought, that was different. It was business that kept Harriet Woodman in Brackshire in August. Fuck Dunnickin and the Earl and Countess of Fraud!

"Business? Frightful. Nothing coming up except bloody Wanstock Manor for the nth time. How's horrible Paradise Farm?"

They had closed like men-of-war under high-spirited captains.

"On the small side."

"Oh, bollocks. Got a chum, have we?"

The archness disgusted Jim.

"It's ground I need, Harriet. If you're going to farm fifty acres, you might as well farm five hundred."

"Look at him, now! Well, as it turns out, a certain other house might be coming up. And we're not talking five hundred acres. Nor five thousand."

Harriet could not quite leave it at that. Her social character cast a backward glance. "Poor Marina," she sighed. "Poor little waggy Marina."

Away Harriet flew, like Azrael in a 4×4, having pronounced her doom on two houses. Jim had no interest in Mount Royal House. It had done for the Bolingbrokes, and now, it appears, it was doing for Charles Lampard. Looking down at the volume in his hand, he asked himself: Now why did I buy this for two hundred of my pounds? The book was the size of a small paperback, bound in brown leather, with a frontispiece portrait of the first Earl of Bolingbroke and the title *An Account of some Pottes or Urnes Lately Found at Haize in Brakeshire*. It began: "In a large Arable Field, lying between *Haize* and *Misselden*, but belonging to *Haize*, and not much more than two furlongs from *Paradise Hall*, the seat of the author of this memorial, divers *Pottes* or *Urnes* were found."

Jim thought it better to read the rest at Paradise Farm.

Later on, what seemed strangest to him was that though the little book had been printed, according to its title page, at the sign of The Swan in Brightwelle in the year 1620, Jim could find no other copy. There was no entry in the electronic English Short Title Catalogue, as the man in the shop had said, nor in the other catalogues of the British Library, the New York Public Library, the national libraries of Scotland and Wales, the Bodleian, the Fitzwilliam or the Bibliothèque Nationale. It might have been that all the other copies had been lost, but that was not at all likely. It might

144

have been that old Francis Bolingbroke had printed just a single copy, but that was perverse beyond reason. Why print if you do not wish to disseminate? Jim felt as if he were holding a piece of rare china, the only survivor of a certain style or shape or dynasty, but now pure gravity, which wished only to be dropped on the stone flags and obliterated.

A Part of the Field being designed to be inclosed, for the Purposes of Improvement, while the Workmen made severall Ditches, they fell upon divers *Urnes*, but being earnest in their work, and *Break-Country* men, as they say, they broke all they met with, and finding nothing but Cinders and a sorts of white powder, not so moist as Chalke but baked and granullar as in a *Tabacco-pipe*, they scattered what they found. Upon Notice given unto me, I went to the Place, and though I used all Care and the Workmen, by Emulation of my Example, did the same, yet were all the *Pottes* broken in the taking out, and many, without doubt, are still remaining in that Ground for Posterity.

Of these *Pottes* none was ever found above Three-Quarters of a Yard in the Ground, whereby it appeareth that in all this time since *Antient Times* the Earth hath little varied in its surface though this Ground hath been Plowed to the utmost Memory of Man.

Out of one of them was brought to me a Silver Penny or *Denarius*, with the Bust of *Diva Venus* on the Obverse side, on the Reverse the Figures of the Emperor and Empress joining their Right Hands with this Inscription *Concordia*. I also received from some Men and Women there present, in return for money of our *Sovereign King James*, Coins of the Emperors Severus and Caracalla each with *Diva Venus* on the Obverse Side.

Some Egyptians digging at a little Distance from the *Urne* Places, in hopes to find something of Value, after they had digged about Three Quarters of a Yard deep, fell upon an Observable Piece of Work, whose Description this Figure affords. The Work was Square, about One Yard and a Quarter on each Side, in Colour Red, solid, without any Mortar or Cement or Brick in it, but of an whole Piece. In this Work were Thirty-two Holes, of about One Foot and a Half *Diameter*. Upon Two of these Holes, on the East Side, some Pottes were found, but broke by the Workmen, being necessitated to use hard Blows for the breaking of the Ground. One fragment of Potte was brought to me, and upon it the Depiction of a Man and a Woman at *Pleasure*.

Bolingbroke had a reputation as an adept and "dabbled in chemistry", or so it was said. John Evelyn reported that the "Wizard Earl" had become convinced that a monk at Brightwell Abbey had been in possession of the philosopher's stone and had, at the dissolution of the abbey at King Henry's order, concealed a quantity of the elixir in the dormitorium wall. Whether he found it or not, Bolingbroke pulled the old abbey apart. Jim wondered if it was this monastic rubble that made the door-cases and the cornerstones at Paradise Farm.

Not having studied the classics at school, he had no prejudice against ancient languages. The Greek alphabet and the rules of Latin grammar he found on an American college website. After an hour's study, he understood that John Walker, when he counted sheep, counted in Latin.

Jim stood before his back door and translated the hexameters: "Francis Boling was the name of the man who built this house and to find out in which Year of Our Lord . . ." It was as if he were not answering the riddle but passing through a doorway into a dwelling in which reality had been twisted out of true.

Even when he had translated all of old Bolingbroke's inscriptions, Jim felt like nothing so much as some lucky archeologist outside a tomb in which the faint light of a torch brought objects of beauty to his gaze, jumbled or smashed beyond repair, but gathered there each for its distinct purpose, and everywhere the glint of gold. In the faint beam of his concentration, there came out of the gloom other objects, partial or broken, that promised profounder information and displaced in his attention the objects in the foreground. If he reached out to touch these things, to take them in his hand, they disintegrated. It was as if some vital element had disappeared, but they remained, poised and in equilibrium, like a slipper with its thread perished or a single cornflower, till he touched them and they fell apart in his hand. In all this time, the first Earl of Bolingbroke hovered just out of view, his Latin — so bland, so poised and lucid-sounding, so neat in its stenography — leading Jim ever further from his starting place.

"What is woman but the confounding of man, insatiable beast, care without cease, incessant combat, a daily drain of money, a tempest within doors, barrier to chastity, shipwreck of the sensual, certain adultery, heaviest weight, deadly viper, property in human form?"

Or:

"Trust not your boat to the waves or your heart to a woman."

Or again:

"A tiger is worse than a snake, a demon than a tiger, a woman than a demon, and than a woman nothing."

The inscriptions were so misogynous Jim could not imagine how Boling had managed to establish his five-hundred-year dynasty. Yet as far as Jim could tell, from the *Dictionary of National Biography* and the diarists of the seventeenth century, Francis Poling (later Boling, and later still Bolingbroke) had no objection to women as company. He married not once but twice, first Lady Bankesia Bankes, daughter of Sir Bankes Bankes of Misselden, and the second time a cheesemonger's widow residing in Fleet Street in

London, a Mrs Fulton. He had fathered twelve children of whom three had survived.

Jim had a thought for which nothing in his life had prepared him. Had old Bolingbroke put up those Latin inscriptions on his upstairs lintels to deter not his wives but his dreams? Was he as haunted as Jim himself? If so, in what relation did Bolingbroke's dream-visitor stand to Jeanie? Or was she Jeanie in an earlier phase of subsistence? Or were they both aspects or manifestations of a long-lived or even eternal phenomenon?

"IN GIRUM IMUS NOCTE ET CONSUMIMUR IGNI."

"Round and round we go and are consumed in the fire."

Jim bought the *Oneirocritica* of Artemidorus of Daldis, in the only edition available on the internet, the Aldine of 1518, bound in indigo and gold, Margaret Roper's copy. Jim could not believe that anybody could pay £10,000 for an old book on the interpretation of dreams in difficult Greek, but paid it all the same, for he was impatient. He said to himself: In place of sleeping, I am reading about dreams.

As he became more accustomed to reading Latin and Greek, these languages began to seem to him not dead or extinct. On the contrary, they were alive. It was the English of the radio and newspapers which was stale and putrid and riddled with dead notions and exhausted meanings. The world of Jim's reading seemed new-made, as if he were setting out into seas that had not yet been mapped and sounded, in which there was some memory of a beginning and no

149

intimation of an end. Jim felt, like Odysseus, that he might sail right off the edge of the world. Towards the end of the *Oneirocritica*, he came upon these sentences: "If a goddess visits a man in his dreams, he will be to himself as a young man or beardless youth. For youth is to manhood as life is to death and this world is to the world beyond."

Jim went to London, setting up in a hotel in the Euston Road that accepted dogs. At the British Library, the volumes he asked for were labelled as pornography, and he was led through a thicket of stares to an isolated desk to read them. He thought: So many girls, day after day, you might even become tired of girls.

How do you find a woman that you have seen only in a dream? Turning the pages, Jim tried to bring to mind the shape of Jean's bosom and the curve of her hips. In the end, he found a short-lived psychedelic magazine called *Zeta*, and there she was on a brass bed in flaming seas, unmistakable, in the summer of 1966; and again, later that year, sunburnt on straw bales in *Girl International*. What distinguished her, Jim thought, was a quality possessed by perfect prostitutes. She posed without the smallest modesty or restraint or regret or pleasure or, even, it appeared, any mercenary need. She did not smile. She had no locality or social class, could as well impersonate a countess as a housemaid, could be virginal or lewd as requested. She was able to complete the secret dreams of every man and, for all Jim knew, woman. There was something else that Jim found hard to put into words. It was as if, beside Jean without her clothes, nothing else had any importance, or even reality. The ordinary occupations of women and men, the day's labour or the bringing up of children, had no meaning. In the world over which Jeanie presided, every encounter of man and woman was crowned with happiness and glory.

Some time in 1967, Jean Thinne was photographed by Mark Neal for the sleeve of Iron Heart's *Leaves of Fire*, bare-bosomed in the fork of the old pollard oak at Paradise Farm. That picture long survived her. Even after Iron Heart fell apart, the view of Jeanie was reproduced on cassettes and CDs and all the afterlife of *Leaves of Fire*, numbering some five hundred million copies. For those who knew nothing else of Jean Thinne, her face and bust were as much of that moment in England as John Hannell's voice or Dick Morton's Flying-V guitar, and partook of their novelty. Jim suspected that the hippy couple in his oak tree were the outriders or pioneers of a new cult of the 1960s which would in time confer on Paradise Farm a worldwide fame. There'll be money in that, he thought, and then just as soon forgot about it.

Fourteen days after *Leaves of Fire* was released, Jeanie was turned away from the enclosure at Royal Ascot for entering without a gentleman escort, hat, gloves, stockings or shoes or indeed anything but a dress she had cut herself from flowered Danron that reached to some twelve inches above the knee. By midsummer 1967, Jeanie Thinne was on the cover of both *Mode* and *Apparel Weekly*, showing only her face. From the Sunday colour supplements, she glared at Jim through a fog of Scottish liqueurs and king-size

151

cigarettes. Hers was a progression from lewdness towards modesty which he suspected was not unique, or even unusual. He also knew, with a worldliness that would have been quite beyond him a week or so before, that this progression reached backwards in time, and that there existed — not in the British Library, oh no, not there — pictures and film stock of Jeanie with which, in comparison, the *Girl International* photographs were demure to the point of virginality. Jim was rather a prude than otherwise, but it was not his feelings of propriety that were offended. For he knew he must travel to Hamburg and Amsterdam, and sift not through library catalogues but through the bins of sex shops on the point of bankruptcy. In these moments, time passed for him in both its aspects, as history and as experience. Jean Thinne was a denizen of his dreams, not the ace model girl of the '60s who married a spiv and topped herself.

London was strange. The ordinary city seemed to Jim to have lost reality. Dazed by old-fashioned pornography, Jim was bombarded by objects of desire. Everywhere were pretty woman, vehicles, clothes and food, or pictures of them. Everywhere were promises of incessant happiness. Everybody seemed on the brink of happiness, which somehow was never attained, or dispersed at the instant of attainment, for the dance went on, in a cacophony of happiness, the vehicles, foods and long-legged girls. Bewildered in the Euston Road, Jim felt he was Tantalus in the *Odyssey*, standing in a lake up to his chin, orchard trees above his head, pears and pomegranates and sweet figs, dying of thirst.

It was as if the whole world were being punished for stealing food from the gods.

Accustomed to listening to the sounds around him, Jim was deafened. He thought the Londoners were shouting at him. He was like that Brazilian princess of the eighteenth century who, coming to London, presumed the shops and squares had been lighted to honour her.

It was as if London was surrounded by a Chinese Wall, through which all the ordinary purposes of the world came in and were transformed into fashions. Everybody was speculating in native art or carrying knives or, in the next moment, adopting orphans. Even the humblest immigrant considered himself to be on view, as if he were a courtier of the ancien régime.

Yet what struck Jim with the greatest force was the Londoners' indifference. People lived in a sort of perpetual middle ground, unaware of the sources of their prosperity or of its consequences. Their city was like an unimproved machine which consumed great quantities of fuel to create, alongside rivers of waste, a little intermittent power. The people themselves were like infants. The food in the shops and restaurants was soft and runny and savourless as if made for babies. The smallest frustration brought rage, the smallest success euphoria. Jim stood on street corners imagining the smell of hay cut from fields beyond the suburbs.

He pulled himself together. He recognised that in just half a year, he had become estranged from his old world and would never again make so much as a penny in business. To punish himself, he walked all the way to

153

City Road. There, in a dirty building with nylon blast curtains, he ordered the financial statements that all corporations, however closely held like Lampard Trust, in return for the inestimable benefit of limited liability, must make available to the public. Among Lampard Trust's many subsidiaries, Jim found a company called Financial Software Ltd. It had neither assets nor employees. While Jim had been playing the farmer, the company from which he had been expelled had been liquidated. Jim could not read a face or a heart, but he could read a balance sheet. He walked out into the street and, with a bow to the shade of "East India" Bolingbroke, called a stockbroker.

In Hamburg, Jim missed Argos so badly that he returned in a turboprop to Brightwell Airfield. Through a porthole scratched and scored by hail, he could make out The Maiden brook, and the old stag-head oak, and the wheat, and the line of church towers. So small a place the earth! At the archive of Brackshire County Council, he studied photographic mosaics made by the R.A.F. in 1946, a short-lived commercial company in 1988, and NASA in 1993. They were recognisably the same landscape, though the hedges had been uprooted to make fifteen-acre fields into fields of five hundred acres. Jim had not come to mourn hedgerows. Once he was familiar with this new point of view, he found nothing.

"Is there anything earlier?" he asked the archivist. "Anything from the '20s or '30s?"

"Well, there's always the German wartime photographs. You'll have to go to Washington for those, or maybe Lambeth."

Jim went back to London, to the Imperial War Museum in Lambeth, where he found a set of aerial photographs taken by the Luftwaffe over several days between 1 and 15 June, 1940. Though black-and-white, they were superior in both clarity and spatial resolution to the mosaic surveys and the satellite pictures. They had been taken at about 20,000 feet by an aeroplane flying straight and level with the optical axis of the camera at right angles to the ground. Jim could make out Paradise Farm and the wheat and the stag-head oak in it. Around the tree were a set of precisely regular marks that, if joined up, would have made a rectangle. Enclosing it at some distance was a larger rectangle, broken by voids at the midpoint of each side.

Jim was baffled. Why had this image appeared in these photographs, and not in those of six years later, or via the flawless lenses and ultra-sensitive film of the NASA satellite? The photographs had been taken on a dull day on which the stag-head oak cast no shadow. Jim knew that summer had been hot, and the Battle of Britain had been fought in brilliant blue skies. He wrote to the National Meteorological Archive in Exeter. In June 1940, he was told, the weather station at Brightwell had recorded 6.2 millimetres of rainfall and 290 hours of sunshine. That was an anomaly; the average for 1971–90 was 50mm of rain and 192 hours of sun. In such a drought, where the barley would be as white as an albino's hair, the small excess of moisture in an ancient trench or the lack of it in the buried remains of a wall or column socket would be like a scream to someone passing overhead.

Now, when he stepped out with Argos, Jim thought to see vapour trails entwined in the blue air. He wondered if the German pilot, when he saw the slashes in the barley at Paradise Farm, understood that those were not airfields or ordnance, but antiquities. Did the analysts back in Rotterdam understand that the thirty-two square marks were the bases or sockets of structures now lost and not the stanchions of a barrage balloon or an anti-aircraft battery? Jim felt that he was shedding his distinctive personality. He had moved out of himself, into the body of the young German pilot, and beyond that into some unimaginable past.

What was here was not an antiquity, but the ghost of it: a trace or clue so buried and suppressed, so obliterated by the plough, that it survived just from the slightest excess of moisture where it lay, history distilled to a droplet of dew. As an item of knowledge, it was at the very end of its existence, passing through time like the light of an exploded star. By fortune, a young German pilot had been there to photograph its final gleaming with his incomparable Leica lens and Agfa film. By a second stroke of fortune, Paradise Farm had passed to Jim, a man with the mental stamina of an ox.

What Jim could not see was the cause of these marks across his land. He assumed there was a cause because there was a cause to everything. If he heard a voice in the dark, there was a person there. If he found a footprint on a beach, a creature had passed that way. If he saw smoke, there was fire somewhere. Experience had taught him that these pairs were invariably conjoined, that there was no voice without person, footprint without foot, smoke without fire. Yet what was this thing in his fields, and what was its pair? In the heart of the smaller rectangle, a tree had grown up or been planted, or a successor tree, or a super-successor. Otherwise, the two axes of the enclosure bore no relation to the pattern of Jim's fields or to the roads or to Hobhouse's pre-enclosure map of 1792, or even to the medieval parish boundary.

Through the window, John Walker had the spring-trap in the stable yard and was prising it open with a scaffolding pole. He seemed to Jim not quite corporeal, like a dream that had somehow endured into the sunlight.

"For God's sake, John," said Jim, standing on the doorstep. "Health and Safety!"

John stood back, hands on his hips. "A shame not to have it working," he said. He was returned, refreshed, from his holiday. "There's money in it. Maybe the Bloody Bone would buy it."

Jim doubted the pub in Haze would really pay to display a man-trap in its saloon bar. "I want you to draw me a map."

John looked evil.

"You're a good carpenter, John. I know you are a good draughtsman. I want you to map the six churches visible from here. I need precise bearings, distances and elevations. If necessary, I'll buy you a theodolite."

"Why did I want a theodolide?"

"You do it your way, John. Please do not draw any other feature but the churches."

John gave him an insolent look, sighed or swore, and abandoned his useful and rewarding project. Jim went back to thinking.

Jim did not trust John Walker and needed to occupy him. Jim was more than capable of superimposing his Luftwaffe photographs on an Ordnance Survey map. He had not the slightest doubt what the outcome would be. It was as if he were at draw poker, and the card that he knew, by the elimination of all competing possibilities, to be an ace, turned over an ace. He was as sure as any man could be that lines drawn through the main axes of the two groups of churches passed through the openings in the outer enclosure, and ended at the midpoint of each side of the inner enclosure. So that was that.

Jim stood on the lawn of Paradise Farm. The country was new oriented. Beneath the lanes and hedgerows, and the main road and sea lanes funnelling people and things into Brightwell, there was a set of older roads preserved in the alignment of the medieval churches and in parch marks that had survived until at least June 1940 and since vanished. Why the churches had been set out in line Jim did not know. It was possible that in the eleventh century, when Haze Church had been built, there had been old roads that were now obliterated. After all, Haze Church had been built only six centuries after the Roman armies had retreated from Britain, but it was ten centuries from the building

158

of the church to the present. So much time has elapsed on this old earth! Even if there was no trace of the ancient roads, the rights of way might have survived in the general orientation of the district, just as the modern City of London preserved in its street map the disposition of Julius Caesar's fortified town.

Or might the churches have been built to extinguish or suppress an older cult, rather as the lime-washed walls and smashed statuary of Haze Church were designed to obliterate the worship of the Virgin and saints after England and its rulers broke with the Roman Catholic religion? Even if all memory had passed away by the Middle Ages, and the antiquities of Brackshire had all been lost, might not a faint superstition still attach itself to certain fields or woods and recommend them as the sites of holy buildings?

Jim halted. He had used the words *cult* and *worship* and *superstition* and *holy* only so that he could pursue his train of reasoning into territory remote from his experience. He was, he knew, proceeding into darkness by the fitful light of his own mental concentration. Yet while he knew that he had supplied the notion of a temple or sacred enclosure only to further his argument, and that it was a mere invention of his imagination, he had, as it were insensibly, been drawn into making use of words as if a temple or sacred enclosure were items of his experience or facts of reputable history or palaeology.

It was a mere habit of mind that everything old and enclosed must have had some ritual purpose. The enclosure might just as well have been a fold for cattle or a rich farmer's villa or some forgotten military installation. With an obstinate effort of will, Jim converted the barley marks into a Roman camp unique for having no civilian remains, or a Roman signal station with no view of the sea, or a Royalist stronghold of the Civil War, or a World War II Type-23 pillbox and anti-tank ditch of which nobody in the district remembered the building, existence or demolition.

Jim fell into a melancholy. If he had not come to Paradise Farm, if Mrs Lampard had laid out parterres or whatever such people did, or McCain had succeeded in uprooting the old oak, or Dark had sold out to house-builders, even this vestige of the ancient past would not have survived.

What other items of knowledge from antiquity were themselves falling into oblivion because there was no young German airman to catch them before they were engulfed? What chances, what sequences of accident, human choice, strokes of good and bad fortune, sunshine and hard weather, what ramifications, what innumerable forks in the road had preserved the Riace Bronzes, say, or the only complete song of Sappho, which begins: "He seems to me like a God the way he sits there across from you"?

What ironies of history! When the ship bearing the two more-than-lifesize bronze athletes had run into difficulties off Reggio or Riace in Calabria, and the captain had cast them into the sea, he must have said to his owners, if he survived: We had to jettison the two bronzes, else the whole cargo and the vessel would have gone down. I am sorry the bronzes are lost. Yet the bronzes were not lost, but, on the contrary, are the only such statues not to be lost, and it was tossing them into the sea that stopped them being lost. For there they lay in the sand, not defaced by iconoclasts or Muslims or melted down for their bronze, till the summer of 1970, when a pharmacist from Rome on a diving holiday saw a bronze arm sticking out of the seabed. Likewise, with the poem of Sappho, what if Dionysius Longinus had said to himself, as he wrote his treatise *On the Sublime*: This poem is as well known as any from the golden age; to illustrate the treatment of sexual passion in great literature I need only quote the first line. But something must have stirred in him, a tremor of fear for the future of Greek civilisation, or an act of piety to a long-dead woman, and he wrote down all sixteen lines, and some monk somewhere copied them out, and another, and another, and another, until a copy ended up in the Vatican Library, where Francesco Robortelli read it in 1554 and printed it. So Sappho passed through this infinitesimal gate into the wide plain of the sixteenth century when everybody was mad for Greek, and she would survive as long as Greek survived or until some new catastrophe brought learning down to a point through which only the most fortunate would pass, or nobody. Jim pulled himself together. He recogised that he could no longer distinguish the past from the future and that, like some fleeing soldier suddenly mindful of his oath, he must turn about to face the present.

It was too late in the season to begin an excavation, but there were all sorts of preparations to be made for next spring. Something of his old business efficiency returned. Jim knew enough physics to be sure that disturbed ground would preserve all sorts of magnetic anomalies. Material that had been burned either lost its magnetism or preserved the magnetic alignment of olden times. He searched for manufacturers of magnetometers and hand-held satellite navigation devices, examined their specifications, talked to salesmen about prices. For the first time in his life, he was glad that he was not indigent and need not haggle over these costly instruments. In conversation, vistas of digital cartography opened before him. Jim saw how he and John would occupy their autumn and winter, preparing the most scrupulous digital model of the site through a mixture of aerial and satellite cartography, boot-leather and geophysics. John would have to part, for a while, at least, with one of his figurines so that Jim could subject it, or rather the crystalline minerals in it, to thermoluminescence dating.

As for the digging, Brightwell Sixth-Form College could do it and cause its name to resound throughout the learned world. In reality, Francis Bolingbroke and John Walker had done the necessary excavation. Now it was just a matter of exposing what was already known. At Paradise Farm, there had been a monumental temple of the goddess Venus, with the epithet *Victrix*, "giver of victories", erected by soldiers of the VIIIth Legion some time in the reign of the Emperor Septimius Severus, or about A.D. 210. Around it had been a suburb with a far-flung industry for making pottery and votive figures and figurines. A similar temple, though at about one fifth of the size, had been excavated at Troisdorf in the Rhineland and another at Adamclisi in Romania. Whether the Paradise Farm temple was superimposed on that of an earlier cult of some British goddess, Jim could not say. What he *could* say was that it was the largest sanctuary of Venus found apart from the colossal temple built by the Emperor Hadrian on the Velia in Rome, and the shrine at the goddess' birthplace in Paphos in Cyprus.

Why had this building left no trace in the memory of the district? Well, of course it had, and in writing as large as an advertising hoarding. Why, of all names, was the brook called The Maiden, and the only piece of old woodland in the six villages to have escaped replanting, Ladies, or rather Lady's, Wood? What else was Temple Farm? These names were as eloquent as if smashed marble columns and pediments lay tumbled in the briars. Why did John Walker count his sheep in Latin? Jim thought: We pass our lives in a fog in which objects are obscure that would be evident to a sick dog. I have brought science and the rule of law to bear on all the phenomena of Brackshire, except my accursed dreams, which were the origins of my investigation and without which I would not have proceeded. Was it the cult of Venus that drew Jeanie Thinne to Paradise Farm and keeps her here to haunt my sleep and harvested fields?

CHAPTER
ELEVEN

A Winnowing Fan

Jim opened the back door on a little girl in a tracksuit who was standing on one leg. She looked scared out of her wits. Jim recognised her as Rose's granddaughter.

"Hello, Tiffany. Can I help?"

She began to speak, hesitated, then plunged in. She said: "Grandmother says can you go to the big house, now, without delay?"

Jim noted her grown-up way of talking. He said: "Is anything wrong, Tiffy?"

"Nan just said you must go."

Jim wondered why he was now at Rose Pledger's beck and call. "Does Lord Bolingbroke need me for something, Tiffy?"

"I don't know," she said and made to run off.

"Hold on, lass," said Jim. "Would you please go to John Walker's and ask him to meet me at the Bothy?"

"Oh no," she said. "I can't. Nan said."

Damn it, thought Jim. What *has* the poor man done? He said: "Please do it, Tiffany. I'll explain to your nan later."

She was gone at the run. From her movement, Jim guessed the tracksuit was an item of fashion rather than of physical training.

He whistled for Argos and climbed into the Land Rover. The starter motor turned over, but there was no ignition. The fuel dial showed a tank of diesel.

"Damn you, woman," he said out loud. He set off on foot, and turned towards the ford, Argos running busily ahead. At the ford, Jim took off his shoes and splashed through. The urns and balustrades of the Bothy appeared and vanished in the trees. A foreboding gripped him and he raced the dog under the stable tower and into the kitchen yard. Why had he not gone to see Jack? It was his damned arrogance. He was certain that he and he alone could solve this mystery and deliver it, unravelled, at his friend's feet. The result was catastrophe. At what looked like the kitchen door, Jim barged in, shouting:

"Mrs Pledger! Mrs Pledger!"

There was no answer. He pushed at swing doors, and emerged into the marble hall, face to face with Jeanie's picture. He did not avert his eyes.

"What do you want?"

Did he expect her to respond to his glance? There she lay, an item of the past, without even a name to bring her down to earth, only an attitude or a gesture. The gesture said: Look at me, for now you may, and take the best of life, for there is nothing else, and the grave makes your projects fruitless. This is the Age of Love, which will have an end, as do all things under the sun, but not for a while yet, not for a good long while.

165

On the first floor, they ran through the enfilade of rooms, Argos sliding on his back claws on the polished boards. The dog led the way up the next flight where they barged into Rose, who was on her way down.

"What's happening, Rose?"

"I had to go," she said, turning side on to pass man and dog. "I did all I could."

"Have you called Dr Mehta?"

"He came."

She carried on down to the landing. She was about to pass out of sight.

"For God's sake, Rose, what did he say?"

The woman flared up. "Don't you God's-sake me, Jim Smith!"

Jim gathered himself. She was at the turning of the stair. In one step, she would be out of sight. "Please tell me what Dr Mehta said, Rose."

"It's just not the same."

Of course it's not the same, you stupid woman! A good man is in agony and a five-hundred-year-old family is going to ground, and all you can think about is how it all appears to you! Jim turned to go up.

She said: "Jack's in the old schoolroom. The doctor said I should tell his family, but I didn't know nobody but you."

"Thank you, Rose. You've done very well. I'm afraid I asked Tiffany to go and find John Walker."

"Well, she won't go. And nor will I."

"No, I suppose not. Why do you hate John, Rose?"

"Because he's sick. You're all sick. Every one of you people."

166

Jim saw no virtue in replying.

He followed his dog upwards. He thought: Why should she stay and watch a stranger die of an infectious illness? Why should she stay to hear the end of this old, old song? The Bolingbroke way of life — part stock-job, part feudal fraud, part antiquarian fantasy — that seemed timeless to the Edwardians, is now so decrepit that in the end one is relieved to see it pass. For the first time, Jim understood that the forms of society change not in open conflict or in pitched battles, but through a steady undermining till in the end the house falls in. For all he knew, Rose had always hated the Bolingbrokes, and so had her mother the kitchen maid and her grandmother the tweeny and her great-grandmother the brew-house under-maid. Well, she had outlived them all. Jim knew he would never see her again at Paradise Farm.

Argos led him into a passageway, which was like nothing on the floor below. It was narrow and dark and never meant to be seen. On the boards were old Turkish rugs that must have been worn low in the public rooms and then retired up here amid a litter of dead houseflies. Jim opened a peeling door on a stack of bentwood chairs at all angles. In the next room were iron bedsteads, a bleached battle standard, a pair of riding boots in their trees, a rack of ladies' dresses in gauze bags tied at the bottom. The next room had pictures stacked against every inch of wall, a giant bronze inkstand, bound copies of some dead periodical, a child's rocking-horse missing its stirrups, but with a tail of real horsehair. These objects seemed to Jim

agitated, restless, ready to go, held in place not so much
by their gravity as by the thread of life still left in Jack,
wanting to disperse and creep into other houses, not so
large nor old, to pubs, landfill, flames. Everything was
in the throes of dispersing, was just waiting for the
signal from Jim. In the gloom of the passage he found a
light switch, but there was no power or no bulb. Ahead
of him Argos had his front feet on the lowest step of a
winding stair. Jim followed the dog to a white door at
the top.

As he turned the door knob on sunshine, Jim knew
he had arrived and also why Jack Bolingbroke had
chosen this room to lie in. Athwart the four windows
was the lead of the pediment and beyond it the park
and lake and a brilliance which must have been the
sunshine off the sea at Brightwell. Beneath one window
was a little table with open schoolbooks on it, and a bag
and pencase at its feet, where Tiffany must have been
doing her homework till the doctor or her grandmother
sent her to Paradise Farm. On one wall was a map of
British colonial possessions at their furthest extent.
Against the other was a white-painted iron bedstead
such as you might once have seen in hospitals and
youth hostels and barracks. Jim turned at last to look at
it. Jack was lying on his back, eyes open to the ceiling,
a sheet pulled up and showing his white legs and the
sores which looked to be a sarcoma. On his bedside
table were medicines and a jug of water. Jim went over
to the bed and took his friend's hand and placed it to
his lips.

He said: "Jack, it's Jim. I'll stay with you now."

Sorrow engulfed him. He thought: I knew you for just half a year, yet we might have been friends for a lifetime. Jim saw Jack slouching down Westchester High Street in his antique school uniform, or seated with his friends before ice-cream sundaes in Miss Adams', or returned in glory after his expulsion in a blue French cavalry cape, red trousers, knee-boots from Herat and a clay pipe.

If Jack heard him, he made no sign.

He imagined Jack in an open car full of mutinous girls, or wrapped in a blanket under a dawn sky at Monterey, or ploughing the bottom field in a straw hat, or going over and over the same difficult sentence in the *Phaedrus*.

On the bedside table, where Rose had made some semblance of order before becoming disheartened, was a phial of something Dr Mehta must have given Jack by injection. It was diamorphine.

He said: "Jack, this torment will not last for ever. You will have peace quite soon. I promise."

The eyes flickered a moment. The mouth opened. Sensing that Jack wished to be moved, Jim with great difficulty turned him to face the window. The thin body was as heavy as lead. The skin was cold and greasy. Breathless, Jim looked up and saw John Walker had come in and was standing in the sunshine.

John advanced, put his hands on his hips, and shouted: "For a sick man, Jack, you don't look half bad." He spoke too loud, as if Jack Bolingbroke were deaf, or a child, or slow-witted. Jim looked up at him, and turned away.

John bellowed: "We'll have you out and about in no time at all, Jack."

Jim did not know what caused John to behave like this. He supposed that behind each death is another, an aboriginal or fundamental death. Had John crept into a dark room as a child to hear someone shouting at a dying man? Well, Jim had no monopoly of silence or his friend. He said: "Would you open the window? So Jack can look out."

The glassy gaze, which had been fixed on the casement, now passed through to where the light was shining off the reedy lake. Jim believed that his friend was on his way. His body would soon cease to hold his spirit which must go on and on.

John shouted: "I tell who I saw today, Jack . . ."

Jim raised his hand. He said the only thing that seemed worthwhile at such a moment. He said: "Listen, Jack. Even deceitful Odysseus, who angered Poseidon, was freed in the end. He brought Tiresias to the trench so he could hear what was in store for him. Jack, you must beach the vessel, and take the best oar you can find and carry it on your shoulder till you come among people that know nothing of the sea and never eat salt with their food, so that our red ships and long oars like wings are outside their comprehension. And this will be the sign, a clear sign that you cannot mistake. You're going to meet another man on the road who will ask you 'Why on earth have you got a winnowing fan on your shoulder?' and then you'll know the time has come to plant your oar in the earth and sacrifice a ram and an ox and a wild boar."

170

Jim stopped because Jack Bolingbroke was moving his lips. Then they stopped moving and a gust or breath rattled his teeth. After a while, Jim closed Jack's eyes and placed a penny between his friend's teeth.

John Walker stood at the foot of the bed. He said: "What did Jack say? At the end?"

" τὰ δ'ἄλλ' ἐν Ἅιδου τοις κάτω μυθήσομαι. "

"I don't understand foreign languages."

"He said, John, in Greek: 'The rest I shall tell those down in Hell.'"

"She won't let him alone."

"Yes, she will, and she'll leave you in peace, too, John. Trust me."

"What can you do? You who never knowed her!"

"When can we harvest, John?"

There was no answer.

"I said, John: When can we harvest?"

Jim turned and saw his employee shaking in the midst of the dead-room.

"John, I need to speak with the woman who comes, whoever she is."

There was no answer.

Jim said: "Perhaps, John, we should make ourselves useful."

John Walker regained his self-control. "I'll see Ernest Jones."

"Is he the undertaker?"

"In Brightwell."

Descending the stair in the darkness, Jim blundered into his dog. Argos was halted, with a paw raised, on the step. The fur along his backbone was hard and erect. Whatever there was, it was something a dog could hear or smell or see.

"What is it, lad?"

Jim could hear nothing. Yet it was as if he were equipped with Argos' animal sense that detected something he could not ignore, a disturbance of the dust or of the lumber in those rooms which were now mobilised. Something or somebody was moving through them, not as a familiar or a denizen, but as an opportune visitor. He sensed that near him was a human being. This person was so afraid that it could not move or speak. It had retreated into a corner where two walls met the floor. It was as if this person were shaking itself to pieces from fear and grief and shame.

"It's all right. I won't hurt you."

The person was a little girl.

"Tiffy? Is that you, girl? Don't worry, it's only Jim Smith. I'll take you back to your nan."

It was not a girl, but a grown woman. In her terror, she had reverted to the helplessness of childhood. Jim's heart melted.

"Please. I won't let anybody hurt you. I'll help you."

There was no sound, except the breathing dog and something that might have been wood pigeons in rustling trees. Yet somewhere about Jim was a trace or vestige, a perturbation of the darkness, or pressure of the air, of which he knew nothing except that it was feminine and mortal and scared to death.

The impression became more faint. It was receding from him.

"Go on, Argos."

The dog stepped down the corridor. He growled.

"Ssh."

The door at the base of the stairs opened onto sunshine. Two men bundled through.

"What are you doing here?"

The men gaped. Jim recognised one of them as the man who had taken his coat at Mount Royal House. Jim's anger was uncontrollable. Jack not half an hour gone and that grubbing Mrs Lampard was snooping round! He said: "Are you armed?"

"I am not at liberty to reveal that."

"Well, I am at liberty, and I can reveal that I am armed and I will shoot you both in your ugly faces unless you get out of here and never come back."

The men stood their ground. "You have no authority here."

"No, that is correct. I have no authority here. I do, however, carry a sidearm which I intend to use." Jim raised his arm.

The men scampered out. "You'll hear about this . . ."

". . . proceedings . . ."

"Yeah yeah yeah." Jim laughed. What's happened to me, he thought. Become such a rough customer all of a sudden.

In the days that followed, Jim fell into a torpor. He would stand for hours, looking out at his wheat, but not seeing it; or walk up and down the rows, pulling up plants and rattling the kernels in his fist for a hint of ripeness. In the midst of this inaction, a black gentleman in a dark suit appeared at the back door. Jim opened the door and the man stepped in and walked through to the kitchen.

"I know my way, thankye," he said.

Of the man's errand, Jim had no notion, only that he had some purpose or profession that required a dark suit, or vice-versa. His Brackshire accent made a contrast with his deep black skin that Jim, a prig in racial manners as in so much else, was reluctant to acknowledge. Perhaps an ancestor had been a Bolingbroke footman, left high and dry and free in Brackshire by the judgement of Lord Kames in *Knight* v. *Wedderburn*: "This man cannot be returned against his will to Jamaica. We cannot enforce the laws of Jamaica, for we sit here to enforce right and not to enforce wrong."

"May I offer you coffee, Mr — ?" Jim hoped, by this manoeuvre, to oblige his visitor to undrape his colours.

"I'll take a glass if I may."

Jim had nothing in his larder to offer the man but Rose's cooking liqueurs. He poured his visitor a tumbler of something glistening and golden. The man drained it off and set it down, but in a provisional manner, as if he would take the second half just so soon as business was complete. He had with him a millboard and a pen.

He said: "Mr Medley was asking if you was wanting plumes."

Jim was at a loss.

174

"Mavis had plumes."

"Well, then, I think Jack should also have plumes."

"And the six, rather than the four, I think."

"I agree."

Jim's visitor looked at him as if to say: This can sometimes be tiresome, but not in your case!

"In the matter of pallbearers, we thought that perhaps you yourself would have wished to accomplish this last office for your friend. You are a strong man, I see."

"Of course."

"And I proposed myself, if I may. As for the other four . . ."

"Perhaps you would be kind enough to ask Mr Medley . . ."

". . . and his two lads and . . ."

". . . and John Walker, if he is at home."

"John Walker?"

"Yes, John Walker."

Now, the visitor seemed to say, I would never describe this work as a pleasure, but when men understand each other, then the business can proceed! Jim saw that long ago the villages had decided on some gypsy farewell for Jack, black horses and nodding feathers and jingling harnesses and heels striking sparks off the roadway and the Medley lads running beside the team, and it was not for Jim to propose alterations. It was for Jim to pay. Jim racked his brains. He said: "I imagine we should have some flowers."

The man beamed. "The womenfolks always wants flowers."

Jim thought: The ambition of the very poorest man is to have a decent funeral, to which all the men of the district are invited, with a good coffin, beer, whisky, cake and tobacco. It is only at that moment that the poor man can be improvident, and for that moment he will stint all his life.

"And something for the mourners to eat and drink."

"Lovely job! I was intending to drop by the Bloody Bone. I'll have a word with Ruth."

Jim felt that something was required of him to press forward the business to its resolution. He said: "Would you like an advance against your costs, Mr — ? If you'll just excuse me a moment."

"Oh no. Heavens no."

The man's eyes fluttered down to the table and back again. Jim rose, went into his larder and retrieved the golden flask.

The man took his stirrup-cup standing. He said: "He was a poor good kind of man, Jack Bolingbroke." He set the glass down. "Not that I'm your way inclined myself, sir."

Jim had an inspiration. "Tell me what happened to Jean Lampard, Mr — "

"That was in Father's time," he said.

Jim waited. The man must accommodate him in just this one thing. Or Jim might say: Lord Bolingbroke once said to me: Don't make a fuss of me when my time comes!

"Lord Bolingbroke once said to me . . ."

"Into thin air. One moment, she's riding over hill and hedge, and the next there's just the horse. Or so

176

Father said. There is persons that says that John Walker knows more than he tells, but Father was not one of them. Father thought pretty Jeanie lost her relish for Mr Lampard and took herself away."

CHAPTER
TWELVE

Funeral Games

When Jim came into the church, the mourners were already seated. They turned, looked at him with the utmost disdain, turned back to the front. They must have had an invitation from somewhere. Jim sat down and put his empty head in his hands.

After a time, he sat upright, seeing nothing in particular, hearing rain, organ music, the swish of vestments, rustling paper, women's heels magnified into eternity. He smelled an overwhelming odour of flowers and, looking up, saw the church was white with lilies. From the pews ahead, whispers fluttered and hissed. Women's hats bobbed. Objects passed from hand to hand. Surely, Jim thought, it was but a moment before the first cigarette was lit. It was as if the mourners were saying: We are not dead. Not today. We are in some pissing backwater called Brightwell for the funeral of old Jack Bolingbroke, who is dead, of Aids, the arse.

Jim had no social curiosity. To Jim, Jack Bolingbroke was his beloved friend. He was the only person Jim had ever called by that name. It had not occurred to him that Jack had a fashionable acquaintance which was now gathered, from London and even further away, in this barn of a church in Brightwell, marooned by the pounding bypass, and athwart the habits of the population, like a rock in a navigation channel. He had expected to be alone, or accompanied by country neighbours. He saw no Harriet or Lampards or McCain. There was a self-consciousness to the Londoners that distracted him.

They seemed to say: But of course you know us. But Jim did not. Indeed, there might have been celebrities among them to make them all feel celebrities. It was enough that they were with their friends, insulated by the rain and wind and the ugly church and unfashionable county, at a rather grand funeral, with the most heavenly flowers you ever saw, where they felt as secure and happy as it was possible they could feel.

Jim tried to make sense of them. He tried to put himself in the place of an indifferent and ignorant spectator. Here was a church in a country town, built a hundred years before by the Bolingbroke family in an attack of prosperous Anglican piety that was not to be repeated. Into it, at mid-morning, there enters a troupe of men and women dressed in the mourning style of thirty years before. The men have scorched grey hair and black coats that had once been expensive. The women have poor skin. They smoke cigarettes.

A more discerning man than Jim would have looked through the mourners' costumes and habits to the gestures and conduct of men and women long buried: of calm men in black topcoats stooped like statesmen among black limousines, and maidens with slim, white fingers and transparent veils. These characters of mourning fought with a temperamental vacancy and inattention. The surface broke. The State Funeral flickered once more into view, then vanished. A man patted his pocket for his flask. A lady checked her mobile for messages.

In commercial society, the signs by which people know where they are or where they are going are brands. Jim drew his notions of personality by diverse paths that wound their way back to television and newspapers. He set no great store by values that were not prices. For an ignorant spectator such as Jim, the antique costume of the mourners no more echoed the severity of diplomats among limousines than the women's dresses commemorated the furious widows of romance. They were simply the fashions of past times.

Jim had this thought: It is not time that first fells us, but history, for history proceeds without taking any notice of our wishes. Those things these people thought so eminently historical, their families and houses and universities, the achievements of their parents and grandparents in war and peace, our Dr this and Lady that, their wide and intact acquaintance, all the triumphs of the English and Scottish middle class, their belief that in all these years events derived significance from their witnessing them, all that had turned to clinker. The badges they cherished and had carried with them over thirty years through flats and houses and villas where all manner of other things had come to grief were no longer badges of anything at all. What mattered was not their own lives but those of other people, both one by one and in mass, and occurred not where they were but in another part of the wood.

A woman slid in beside Jim, close enough to touch. He looked up at a powdered cheek, which was to be kissed, so he kissed it. The cheek was cold beneath the powder and brittle as an autumn leaf. For an instant, Jim felt the ghost of his friend. She had Jack's silhouette, long neck, long legs, long hair, no bosom or hips. With this lady, too, there was that hint of dissipation as if she, too, had heard the chimes at midnight, or once seen her two lovers greet each other on some pavement of Mayfair. Jim wondered if she were Jack's sister who, finding it disgraceful not to have met her brother's last friend, acted as if she had known him all her life. In her gloved hand, she had a book with a red binding and a gold top to the pages. The paper was as cold and dry as her skin. She said: "We thought maybe you might read something." She looked round the church in misery.

Not sister, for Jack had no sister. Could Jack have had a wife, perhaps for not very long and in times when preferences in love were not so exclusive or sectarian? Or in search of an heir of his body? Jim recognised that he knew almost nothing about his friend. Jim's mind went out to meet this lady, as if on a window ledge.

"I'd be honoured to read something for Jack, Lady Bolingbroke."

"Jane. They're all coming on to the Bothy after," she said. She turned her weeping face on Jim. "Bad luck, Jim Smith. You're in charge."

What had conserved these people in the state of thirty years ago? They remembered things rather as a man, falling asleep on a long journey, wakes with no notion of time passed. They remembered Jack in his salad days, not the years of misfortune, obscurity and illness. The intervening years had made only faint impressions. Had they all been abroad, or in prison, or struck down by some mysterious sleeping sickness from which a new drug had suddenly woken them? Or were they pickled in snobbery and dividends? Jim knew nothing of heroin and did not hear what the hats and coats were saying: "We are junkies, old boy, you must have guessed, old man, or didn't you find it odd, the susurration, the girls on their mobiles, the banknotes passing from hand to hand, the purple school bus at the graveyard lych-gate? Didn't you know — as, in fairness, we didn't until today — that Brightwell is home to a thriving trade in heroin: at the Black Ram upstairs, in Mudgwells' car park, and that good old purple school bus?"

"Smith! You're on."

With thoughts such as these, and others, Jim stepped up to the lectern. He let the book fall open, looked down at the hats and the spume of white flowers. He saw lilies and white cattleya orchids on the altars and side-altars and window ledges and organ loft and tied to the bench ends. Here were more flowers than all the shops of Brightwell could have gathered, or Chipstable. They must have exhausted the florists even of Chelsea and South Kensington. There was to the flowers nothing of soil or sunshine, only of money. They were money that had exchanged its permanence for mortality, for it was money that would flourish and then die with the stink of the abattoir. Who had donated these flowers, Jim did not know, except that it was a person who could express his, or rather her, sentiments only through excess and expense. There was something infantile about the display as if mere profusion might somehow bring Jack back from where he was. Jim patted the devil's cloud away with the book, which was an anthology of verse.

Jim looked down and saw that the heads were drooping. The poem before him was called "The Defeated". He began:

> In battles of no renown
> My fellows and I fell down,
> And over the dead men roar
> The battles they lost before.

Jim drew courage from the sound of his voice in the church. He felt at ease in his dark suit. His eyes swept the dozing faces.

> The thunderstruck flagstaffs fall,
> The earthquake breaches the wall,
> The far-felled steeples resound,
> And we lie under the ground.

So this, he thought, is one way to deal with mortality: to turn it into a ceremony, in which emotion is indulged, but only to an extent where it is seemly.

183

Those who loved Jack endeavour to restrain their grief to the same pitch to which those who knew him only by acquaintance will raise theirs. All this is seemly, except those accursed white flowers. Dazzled by the unvarying whiteness, Jim felt the funeral pass beyond affected gravity into something else — authentic grief — and he must steady himself.

> Oh, soldiers, saluted afar
> By them that had seen your star,
> In conquest and freedom and pride
> Remember your friends that died.
>
> Amid rejoicing and song
> Remember, my lads, how long,
> How deep the innocent trod
> The grapes of the anger of God.

He came to the end, shut the book, and stepped down among the faces, which snapped upwards. The faces seemed to say: Excellent choice of passage and, if we may say so, well read. In the pew, the widow took Jim's hand and held it in her cold gloves.

They buried Jack in the rain. Jim walked to the graveyard wall where the undertaker, the Medleys and John Walker were standing. The boys had smart new black bowler hats. John, tieless and dishevelled, was smoking a cigarette over the wall.

"I hope you will all be coming over to the Bothy. Jack would have wanted you to have a drink with him."

The boys smirked.

The undertaker spoke up. "We are all taken care of, thankye, Jim."

"Good."

Jim walked back to his car and drove behind his windscreen-wipers to the Bothy.

"You jammy bugger!"

"What?"

"You big pig! Jack left you *Venus*."

Jeanie looked down, as if from Olympus, on a riot. The guests, embayed in the fumes of tobacco smoke and alcohol, the clatter of heels on marble, the distant ceiling with its clouds and bosomy nymphs and the tumbling rain, seemed as secure and happy as it was possible to be. Jack is dead, they seemed to say, the prat, whereas we . . .

"The flowers in the church were lovely, Jane."

"Nothing to do with me."

Lady Bolingbroke held her glass with a certain lack of expertise, as if it contained something she took only at burials.

"What was that bit about grapes at the end?"

"I think what the poet meant was that the world needs losers for God's will to be done."

"The bastard," Lady Bolingbroke murmured. "God, I mean." She drifted away.

Jim, too, had slipped his mooring. In the centre of the hall, the young girl he had seen in the old oak at Paradise Farm was standing, surrounded by men. She seemed to Jim as happy as she could be. It was she, at age thirteen or fourteen, not Jane Bolingbroke or the celebrities, who was the queen of the funeral. The men bent forward at the waist to catch her every word and look down her dress front.

"Where the hell are we?"

A pretty woman glared at Jim. His appearance in the church pulpit seemed to have made superfluous the laws of British acquaintance and introduction.

"The Bothy. Jack's house . . ."

"No, I mean, where are we, precisely?" She looked at Jim as if he were a servant.

"Brightwell."

"And?"

"Brackshire."

"And?" She made a repetitive gesture.

"The back of England."

"At last!" she said. She looked about as if to say: How long does it take some people to establish an uncontested matter of fact! How can one bear the pettifogging slowness of reality!

It seemed to Jim that the mourners knew no more of the geography of England than of Russia east of the Urals. They had come to Brightwell down long roads or in rattling railway carriages, where they had dozed or slept. Sometimes they woke to a place name on a station platform, or a sodden field of cut wheat, a canal bridge, castle, retail park, electricity pylons, and knew that they were neither at home nor at their destination and could return to the guarded realms of sleep.

The woman looked up at the portrait and sighed. "Poor Jeanie."

Jim took his cue. "Were you friends?"

"I was her friend."

The sentence was altogether too refined for Jim. If you were her friend, was she not yours?

"In a way, I was responsible for her success."

I'm sure you were.

"I introduced her to Steve."

"Steve?"

"Of Iron Heart."

Jim permitted this historic claim to be lodged. He said: "Have you seen her?"

"Not for years and years." That's enough of slutty Jean Thinne, thank you. "I heard she married yet again, a Russian or an Arab, was it? Lost her looks."

"Well, it's a long time."

"Centuries!"

Their conversation had attracted interest.

"Jack had everything!" a man bawled. He might have been in a saloon. "Money, looks, a house! Whereas we . . ." His eyes fell on Jim.

"Hi, I'm Simon."

His eyes fell again on Jim.

"Well, well," he said. "It's you, is it? You've got a bloody nerve."

Simon squinted at Jim in a blend of fear and belligerence. The mourners, it seemed, had long but inaccurate memories. It was as if Simon harboured some resentment against a man resembling Jim. This resentment had lodged in his mind for years and years, against the moment that such a man came past, where it could drop down on him, like a tick above a jungle ride.

"I think you are mistaking me for somebody else. I'm Jim Smith."

"Don't be so ridiculous. Nobody's called Jim Smith." Simon looked round in pleasure. He was beginning to enjoy his funeral.

A woman slid Jim's arm through hers. She handed Simon a glass of whisky. She squeezed Jim's arm against her bosom. "Well, I think it's a very nice name."

There was only so much of this that Jim could endure. He sensed that there was already prepared for him an invitation to the troupe, which was open to anybody who could pay his way, and something over his way.

A waiter in a black coat tugged at Jim's sleeve. "Alcohol," he said.

"What do you mean?"

"Want alcohol."

"Who said so?"

"Lady." The waiter pointed at the roaring widow.

Jim approached Lady Bolingbroke through the surge. She shouted: "We need more wine, Jim."

"Shouldn't these people go home?"

"No, they shouldn't. Don't be so fucking middle class, Jim Smith. Jack would kill you if he heard you."

Jim found Jane Bolingbroke and her hospitality quite alien. He pulled himself together. "I'll bring some wine."

Jim breasted his way through the throng and pushed open the cellar door. The waiter, who on Jim's enquiry turned out to be Ukrainian, was at his back. This time the cellar was damp, and the rain fought with the murmur from the party. As his eyes became used to the gloom, Jim saw, on the white-washed bin where he had left them half a year before, the two wine glasses that Jack and he had drunk from. Hades and Dionysus, said Heraclitus, are the same. Death and wine εἶναι τὸ ἴδιον.

Jim heard the stamping of feet above his head. He felt, for the first time, that the characteristic and permanent companion of his life, for which he had no name unless it were his *hardiness*, had passed its high tide and had started to ebb. Jim thought: I did not want to come here, and now I have come I do not want to leave.

"This O.K." The waiter had found a wine called Domaine de la Romanée-Conti. The label read 1959, but Jim thought the mourners were lucky to have anything at all. "*Absumet heres*," says Horace. Your heir will guzzle the Caecuban you locked up with a hundred keys and stain the pavement with the proudest vintages. Jim picked up a case.

"Four pieces."

Jim shouldered a second and climbed the uneven stairs.

As for the guests who had dozed through thirty years of British history, was that so very reprehensible? Was it so much worse than what Jim had done with his life, or Jack, or Charles Lampard or Tim Woodman's two grandfathers and all those people he had met who had barricaded themselves in their pastimes to keep out the siege engines of oblivion? What had Jim achieved with his life, possessed as he was of knowledge such as is

189

given to just one or two mortals in each generation? They all would lie together below ground, hoggledy piggledy.

Jim delivered the wine and left the house to see to his poor dog.

"Busy, busy," said Simon, as Jim took his leave.

Outside in the stable yard, Jim saw the purple school bus and recognised that Brackshire had passed through an alteration. The funeral, and the tastes and habits of the mourners, were like some ship that had beached in a desert region and for a generation would supply the native people for seventy miles in each direction with iron nails and canvas and copper and hemp, and pleasure of a new complexion and bitter sorrow and unfathomable pain.

CHAPTER
THIRTEEN

Lampard at Bay

The rain was beating down by the time Jim set off from the funeral. It splashed up waist high off the clay drive and sparkled in the sunshine. In the sheets of water on the road, patches of cloud and blue sky were turned upside down. The sky beneath the wheels made Jim think he was flying. A double rainbow ran right through him.

The ford was awash with brown, but Jim fought through it. As the car righted itself, he saw a man leading a horse. The man was hunched down in his jacket, collar up, bowler hat pulled down to his ears. The horse, black in the rain, was lame in its offside foreleg. Jim's stomach tightened as he slowed the car.

Charles Lampard was alone. Without the baying hunt around him, or the paraphernalia of attendants and protection, he looked petulant, bewildered and wet.

Jim wound down the window and let the rain blow in. "You can stable the mare with me, if you like. I'm just round the corner. I'll drive you home."

Lampard spun round in the rain, but did not recognise Jim.

"Pulled up lame," he said. "Lost the field. Bloody McCain . . ."

He moved his head and rain poured off the brim of his bowler. It was as if he were talking not to Jim but to history. As for McCain, Jim wondered what he was up to. He said: "I'm just round this corner. I'll go first so the mare doesn't shy."

"I'll see to Gordon McCain."

In his utter frustration — at the rain, at horses — was some rivalry with McCain that was either not confined to the hunting field or had just become manifest there. Jim concluded, as he was sure Lampard had not, that the man's dominance in this district was not God-given, and that, in the slow revolutions of Brack Country time, just as Lampard had displaced Jack Bolingbroke so also might he be displaced.

"And that bloody little Duke of Pisshooks running at the fences with all the women wagging their tits at him."

Jim watched in his mirror as Lampard plodded forward in the rain. Jim was excited by the thought that they were quite alone. They had been seen by nobody. He could pay Lampard back for ruining his business without anybody being the wiser. The villages by now would be dead drunk on Jim's beer, infants comprised. The mare would hobble back, foaming and caught on her reins, to Mount Royal House, and little Miss Madam would be thrown back onto the marriage market. Jim shook off the fantasy. What on earth was putting such thoughts in his head? He who had never wished to hurt a fly? Ahead, the rain began to drum and bounce off the drive, and the house appeared in flashes, stained by the tumbling water. At the back door Jim waited, then took the reins of the mare.

"I owned this house," Lampard said, turning his wet face to the house and then just as quickly turning away.

Everything, Jim thought, must be under his thumb. Jim said: "Go into the kitchen and dry off while I stable the mare."

"Keep her," Lampard said, but without conviction. Jim supposed he was so enclosed and protected by his employees that he could not talk to a neighbour.

Jim walked the horse into the stable, took off the saddle and bridle, dried her flanks and shook down some of Bramble's hay. In no hurry to return, he looked at the mare's fetlock and found a deep gash, as if cut by a knife.

"So who could have done that to you?"

In all his life, he had never seen such a proud and willing horse.

He washed the wound and sprayed it with the tetramycin he used for the lambs. The blue stain on the handsome fetlock looked bucolic and poverty-stricken.

Lampard was seated facing the stove in the kitchen, his coat and hat off. Behind his head, on the table, a kitchen knife stood on its point. There was blood on the point and on the shaft. It quivered, in a pocket of light, defying the laws of nature or rather abrogating them, and Jim knew, with an unbearable relief, that whatever he was to do, whatever he had promised Jeanie in his dreams, he would not do it. He cared not at all that

193

Lampard had robbed him of his company and his good name, for he had no use for them. His honour and credit in business, which had sustained him up to that moment and alone compensated for his hard upbringing and solitary life, now meant nothing to him. Jim lunged for the knife. It spun and clattered to the stone flags. Lampard turned round.

"Come next door," said Jim. He stood above Lampard, and escorted him into the little sitting-room and closed the door. "I'll light the fire and get you a cup of tea."

"Just give me your mobile."

"Use the normal phone."

"It's dead."

The prig in Jim was surprised that Lampard would touch his property without asking. He turned and picked up the receiver to silence. A dead telephone made him think he was listening to outer space. He said: "My mobile needs charging. I'll run you back. Will you send a box for the mare in the morning?"

"What?"

Jim gave up.

Yet Lampard was inclined to talk. His routine was disrupted, his entourage scattered, communications with his staff cut, his wife . . . well, his wife could wait for once in her little life. Perhaps Lampard treasured his moment of masculine peace.

"I bought this place off McCain in the '60s. Fucking crook had taken it off Jack Bolingbroke for eight thousand quid."

Jim let him run.

"I lived here with my first wife. She died. And that . . ."

"I'm sorry."

Patience!

"You just wouldn't begin to understand."

Patience!

They sat and listened to the fire and the rain.

Then Lampard continued. "Does the name Jean Thinne mean anything to you?"

"A name to me, that's all."

"You're too young to remember. She was something. It was like she burst on London in those years, the early 1960s, and nothing would be the same. Before her, women looked like bloody duchesses and here comes Jeanie . . ." He put his head in his hands.

"Was she a model or something?"

"A model? Where have you been? She was the goddess of her age. Every girl wanted to look like her and every bloke to take her out."

"And she married you," said Jim. Something out in the hunting field had hurt Lampard in his masculinity. Jim saw, in a flight of social imagination that even dull and solitary men sometimes achieve, Emilia Dark, erect on her side-saddle, jumping across the path of the heir to the British throne. So, thought Jim, that handsome Mr and Mrs Dark have found another lamb to shear.

"I was so damn cocky in those days. I was running properties for Jack Dilly, mostly in White City and Shepherd's Bush, ratting or firing out the old dearies and running up . . . Used to park my MG on the pavement above Stricklands, gave the copper a fiver to watch it. There was absolutely nothing we couldn't do, we were going to take over this bloody country, shake out the snobs and the deadbeats and the Establishment queers. The girls did not know what had hit them."

"So what brought you back to Brackshire?"

"Jeanie. She was friends with that painter man, Bolingbroke's boyfriend. I bought her this dump so she could play at farming."

"She didn't die, did she?"

Jim had wanted to provoke him. Lampard continued, hunched in his seat.

"You know nothing about it."

It was as if something had altered in Lampard to rob him of his power and self-assurance. He said: "Do you believe in ghosts?"

"It sounds as though you do."

They had come much further than Lampard had intended. He shook himself as if to dissolve the holiday atmosphere and its limited and temporary mingling of social degree. Yet he continued seated. He said: "Do you do your own investments?"

Well, well, well, Jim thought. The fellow is looking for capital. What on earth for?

"Yes."

"Dick Dark has come up with something interesting."

My, my, my. Who'd have thought it?

Jim said: "You have already smashed one of my businesses. I'm in no hurry to let you do it again."

Lampard looked up. If Jim had expected embarrassment, or contrition, or shame, he saw none of those emotions. He saw a leer of pleasure on Lampard's face. Jim thought: This man likes a fight.

"Remind me of its name. And yours." Lampard leaned back in his chair.

"Finsoft. Jim Smith."

"You're better out of it. When I looked at it, there was nothing there." As well as bullying, Lampard could do blandishment. He would speak as an elder businessman to a younger. He said: "Let me give you a word of advice, Jim Smith, based on forty years in business. Never form an attachment to a line or a product. They are just sources of cash. Now, do you want to invest or not?"

Jim would have said, had planned to say: But I have! I have sold five million Lampard Trust ordinaries short for delivery on 1 January. If you wonder why your shares are falling, it is because I have set in train a bear raid that you will not be able to withstand. If the shares fall a further 15 per cent, you will be in breach of your banking covenants and somebody, without an attachment to a line of business or a product, will put Lampard Trust into Administration. If Lampard Trust survives, which I believe it will for it has some franchises, it will be without you.

Yet Jim did not care any more. Something in the last weeks or days had sharpened his moral perception, as if a film or veil had been lifted, and he could now better understand the propriety of his motives. The bear operation, that had seemed to him in London so bold and just, was the action of a braggart. There are certain claims that a man can make that, though true in fact,

197

will always sound like boasts. That is because the purpose of those statements is not to tell the truth but to display or promote the self. Jim wondered where he had learned his new scruples. It was surely not in the company and conversation of John Walker. It was as if he felt obliged to justify himself before a spectator who was unusually good and unusually wise and, just to complicate Jim's task, pretty as hell.

Lampard Trust was failing not because of Jim's short sale, and the pick-a-back trades from his scum of a stockbroker and that scum of a stockbroker's scum friends, but because of Charles Lampard's inattention. No doubt, as the business unravelled, and Russian nickel turned as bad as the Venezuelan tar sands, something in the core of Lampard Trust would take on the character or nature of a fraud. That is what usually happened with failing businesses. What begins in carelessness ends in embezzlement. That all lay in the future. Jim would call his stockbroker and unwind his foolish transaction.

Jim said: "No."

There was the smallest delay before Lampard stood up, as if for a moment he had become conscious of his years or could no longer be bothered. In his hard look, there was no residue of this weariness or senescence, but Jim had seen it, as a sniper sees a match flare.

Lampard said: "You said you'd drive me back to Mount Royal."

"I did." Jim whistled for Argos, and they set off through the rain.

Mount Royal House was lit up like an aircraft carrier. In the faint but almost phosphorescent wake of his conversation with Lampard, the place seemed to Jim altered, no longer a palace, more a mortgaged off-season hotel. For all its massy columns and pediments, it was just a gamble which had not paid off. At an upstairs window, a woman was standing, both arms raised to draw a pair of heavy curtains. The light was behind her, and low down as if from a bedside- or dressing-table lamp, and shone through her brushed hair and the fine muslin or organdie of her nightgown. So, Missus, thought Jim, I shall know next time not to mistake you for a man. Jim left Lampard to his shapely second wife and, in an access of solitude, came straight away.

As he came in sight of Paradise Farm, the house seemed to bend and creak. Beneath the roar of the rain, Jim heard the glass of a bedroom window splinter and tinkle down on the gravel walk. Then another window burst outwards, and another and then the whole front, as if under assault from twenty thousand people. All around the vehicle were falling sheets of glass. Then there was rain, and the creaking of shards in the windows. Jim opened the door, lifted Argos and carried him over the splinters, head well back so the dog would not lick his face.

Jim said: "Somebody's not best pleased with us. We'll sleep in the stable with the mare, lad. I don't believe we'll ever sleep in Paradise Farm again."

CHAPTER
FOURTEEN

Recognition

Lampard sent for his hunter early. Jim had slept with Argos in the stable, and he regretted the dust on his overalls and the straw in his hair as he watched a four-wheel-drive vehicle pick its way down the avenue, pulling a horsebox. It was as if the driver were not used to such a conveyance. On the bonnet of the car was a mascot of a racehorse and jockey, the cap and silks enamelled in green and purple. Perched high up behind the wheel was a woman in a head-scarf.

How laborious is the display of wealth, thought Jim. Such immense and toilsome contrivances and all for such temporary and paltry effect. He held up his hand, and then opened it to indicate the broken windows and the shivers of glass catching the early sunshine. The cavalcade stopped with a bump. The driver's door swung open and Mrs Lampard descended.

Jim was at a loss for a moment, surprised both by her boldness in coming, and by her costume. She had on dark glasses, and a man's shirt, and baggy pants of an expensive cavalry-brown, and boots to the knee. She had put on no make-up. It was not so much an incognito as a suppression of femininity, as if this part of the country were not quite safe for a young wife. Or was it that to have owned Paradise Farm, even if not at the same time as Jim Smith, hinted at an adventitious intimacy that the man might exploit?

She saw the broken glass and gaping windows and jumped.

"Lightning," said Jim. He had better things to do than cover up for malignant Immortals.

Mrs Lampard watched while Jim reversed the horsebox into the stable yard, brought the mare up, unlatched the box and led her in. The mare went in like a Christian. Mrs Lampard looked on in a vacancy of mind. It occurred to Jim that she had never handled a horse. She was not in any sense a countrywoman. Can't ride, thought Jim, can't drive; what can she do? He latched the tailgate and straightened.

"If you don't mind waiting here, I must bring something from the house. I'm afraid there's broken glass indoors."

"Thank you. I must leave. The vet is coming."

"Walter Medley was kind enough to come up, and he cleaned and bandaged the wound. Your husband needs to speak to Walter about what caused it."

"I hardly think that's necessary," she said. "Will you send . . ."

"No, I will not." Jim was tired from his vigil in the straw. He said: "Please wait here."

"I must go . . ."

"Just do as I ask, will you?"

She trembled at the order. Jim lowered his voice a tone: "The dog will guard you, and anyway I carry a handgun."

He caught a glimpse of the face of a frustrated child, but he could not be bothered. Marina Lampard had come to embody all that he most disliked about women. So ruthless they were, in the pursuit of the most misguided purposes, and so deceitful. When he came out with John Walker's map of the churches, she was still standing, Argos seated on his haunches beside her, the door to the vehicle open. Fine taste in people you have, hound, thought Jim. He looked straight into her dark glasses and said: "You came here for something other than the mare, otherwise you would have sent one of your people. I don't know what it is that you want, but I'll tell you what I know, which isn't much. Unless it's something else altogether," Jim added for good measure, "in which case, I can't help you."

Her face blazed. Jim had the reaction he had sought, but found that he did not want it after all. He felt he had been struck in the chest and, looking down, seen blood spreading over his shirt. Jim understood, in shock, that he did not dislike Marina Lampard, but, on the contrary, he liked her very well and better than any mortal creature, and had done so since the instant he saw her trembling in the entrance hall of Mount Royal House. His anger and contempt were, as it turned out, symptoms of a mere frustrated masculinity that he had kept under the most strict control for a dozen years, but had now mastered him.

Jim could accept defeat from a woman. That was nothing. Jim Smith was a man, just like other men, ruled by his heart or his prick, who must assemble from the first pretty face he saw ordinary visions of hearth and happiness. It was his own absolute incompetence that struck him down. How could he be so ignorant of himself and the world that having at last found a person to love he could only insult her? What sunk him so low was the sensation that he was as he had been in his most dreadful period fifteen years ago, without any addition to his character and knowledge from having travelled the world, and survived a pitched battle and a bad wound, and made a fortune in business, and rescued a famous house and found a great antiquity. It was as if he had been returned to his original nakedness and stood injured before this pretty woman. If he could but just staunch the bleeding at his chest, which he sensed was doing him no kind of good, then he would turn away out of her sight.

Jim needed to act. He resolved that he could not go on as he was, his heart-strings snapped and useless as a smashed guitar, or live in this place and country. He would get rid of his property — had always so intended, had no use for it — and would set off, as he had once before, with nothing, not in pointless flight but like a dervish he had once seen in a village near Merv, well armed and peaceable and in his holiday clothes, living on charity or a little thieving.

This plan, so practical and businesslike, brought Jim no comfort for it did not address his capital problem, which was this: he had injured beyond restitution a woman who had come to him, not because she wanted to come to him, but because she had nowhere else to go.

Who was raging. "How dare you speak like that to me? You bastard. What have I ever done to you to make you speak to me like that? Answer me, you bloody bastard or I'll kill you."

Her face was an agony to him. To look at her brought on a vertigo, as if he were standing on a ledge ten thousand feet up. He wanted to fall and, in falling, to lose the pain of looking at her, but at some penalty that he could not imagine. She had her hand raised to strike him across the face. It was her left hand. She was left-handed. Jim felt that if she hit him, there where her hand would fall, on the right temple between cheek and ear, the blow would knock the last sense out of him.

"Answer me, damn you!"

Jim lowered his eyes and said the only thing left in his head: "Because I didn't know, Marina."

He looked up into Mrs Lampard's face. She was bewildered. Resolved to fight, she had not expected surrender. She had kicked with her fine feet at a door and it had fallen open. Then she must have heard something in what he said. Her hand dropped to her hip. The blush receded from her cheeks. Her lips parted. Jim saw, in a stupor, that if he liked Marina Lampard, it was a mere preference in comparison with how she liked him. Something brushed his heart. It was the touch of a passionate nature at the absolute limit of its strength.

Now he saw why Marina Lampard had come to him dressed as for Friday prayers in the women's gallery of the congregational mosque of Burayda. Faithful wife and mother, she was determined that whatever business she must have with the man at Paradise Farm, she would keep it free of all entanglements of sex; but, in dressing with such modesty, she revealed her suppressed reveries. She had buttoned and laced and tied so comprehensively because, at a level some distance below her moral consciousness, she considered doing the reverse. Jim understood that Marina Lampard loved him as no person had ever loved him, more even than his mother.

The disordered events of the days and weeks fell into place. Those objects of their association, the dog carts and sundials and horseboxes of their correspondence, were not distractions from the story but the story itself. They were expressions in the object world of the secret agitation of their hearts. Beyond the register of the ear, there was a clamour that would be heard and had been heard. It was that exhilaration or euphoria that Jim had felt amid his terror that night of the dinner party at Mount Royal House and again in the barns at the Brightwell Show, which was his insurrectionary heart.

Staring into her shaded eyes, Jim marvelled at the force and ingenuity of love that could find its way across fields and woods, past waving wheat and hedgerows full of dog-rose-hips, through torrents of tumbling glass from a woman to a man and back again. They were two of the most obstinate people who had ever lived, and yet they had found each other. That they had chosen each other was certain in all time and all places for it did not depend on anything that anywhere existed in the world. It was like a figure in geometry. Love, which had taken over their present and future, now wished to demonstrate that it owned their past. It was for Marina that Jim had lived as he had lived, had kept his heart intact through the deserts and office parks of his existence, had swallowed his pride. Happiness, a novel sensation and yet beyond doubt authentic, radiated out from her and engulfed him. It was as if Jim found himself in a mountain landscape and the sun broken through to illumine fields and villages of happiness.

To see him better, Marina Lampard took off her dark glasses. There was no sign of feminine triumph in her eyes, or of conquest. If anything, there was surprise as if, after a lifetime of being mistreated, she did not know what to do with kindness. The vertigo that Jim felt became unbearable. To know that her face existed for him, to admire and touch and kiss, whenever he wished, from this moment on, swooped at him on his pinnacle. She reached out to touch him as if to deaden with her fingers a ringing glass and save a sailor's life.

Jim took a step towards her and his new world disintegrated. It was as if a metal sheet had fallen from heaven and cut him in two. Beneath his shirt, his skin was cold. He became aware that Marina and he were not alone, invisible, cocooned in their longing for each other, out of the world. He saw that in fighting her dominion over him, in so wilfully misreading her character, rejecting her shy approaches and insulting

206

her to her face, he had also been trying to protect her. He saw that if he touched her, even gently, the way the dead touch each other on the grave monuments from Palmyra in the old Beirut Museum, he would kill her stone dead; as dead as Jack Bolingbroke was dead. His passion for her was just one more curse — the lamed horse, the knife upended in the air — in Jeanie's implacable vengeance against Charles Lampard. Jim took a step back.

Mrs Lampard was perplexed at his change of heart, and humiliated. Jim gestured for her to sit on the bench. Her shoulders, which only wanted to be enfolded in his arms, started pettishly. Then a shiver went through her and she sat on the iron seat. Jim remained standing. He said: "In ancient Greece there were places where a mortal could descend from the light into the Underworld. One was at Delphi in Attica. Another was at the temple of Zeus at Dodona in what's now Albania. A third was at Didyma near Ephesus. A fourth was at Cumae, near what is now Naples. Even in modern times, where so much has been forgotten about the world, there are places where the spheres of time and eternity touch and intersect. Even in busy cities, on a certain street corner, by a kiosk selling the *Evening Standard*, or an office building where call-centre workers smoke on the steps at noon, or in the carpark of a commuter railway station, there might be one of these passages into the world of the dead. Marina!"

Mrs Lampard was daydreaming. She had untied her scarf and was shaking down her fall of dark hair. Jim's heart faltered. She froze.

"Please go on," she mumbled.

She raised her face. Jim's head swam. Her hair, with its glimmers of red, was something of which any woman would be proud, and yet it was just one of Marina's beauties. He thought: Good thing, Marina, that Lampard locks you up for you would divert a parade, empty a department store, cause a passenger ferry to come down on its beam ends. You are without doubt one of the most beautiful women of modern times. He saw that she let down her hair so he could see it, that it belonged to him, just as his lawns and woods, and fields, and old house he had laid out to show her. He felt that he could endure eternity in Hell just for the touch of her cheek. He was sure that she would give her life to him for the certainty that she had once been loved in the world. It was for him to act the man and show restraint for both of them. A rebellious thought swam into his mind: Of all mortal women, Marina Lampard, you have by far the nicest tits.

So what are you doing about them, mister?

Jim said: "In this part of the country, everybody knows that the old churches are built in alignment, generally but not always in groups of three. For example, Tregawn — Witchbourne — Bablock. Or, in this direction, Misselden — St Roche — Haze. Everybody knows also that each of these churchyards contains an old oak tree, and some people think they are as old as the churches. It was Jack Bolingbroke, or maybe his father or his mother or his grandmother or the stable groom, I don't know, who wondered whether the trees were not planted by the churches, but, as it

208

were, the churches planted by the trees. Also that the specimens we see today might be successors to yet older trees that take us back into antiquity. Jack surmised, but could not verify because of his blindness, that by projecting the line made by the Bablock group to a line projected beyond Haze tower, there might be a place of some significance to the ancients. I have found that those two lines intersect at Paradise Farm. To be precise, at that oak in the pasture."

They turned their heads together and looked at the oak, gleaming in the sunshine. After a while, he stole a glance to the side and found her looking at him. She was laughing.

Harriet Woodman said you were gay.

But you know better.

Not conclusively.

Jim did not want to talk about ancient temples. He wanted to look at Marina's face and carry it with him the rest of his life. Happiness, incarnate in this lion-hearted woman, had come too late. In his daze, a thought kept repeating itself: Why am I not blind? Why am I allowed to see Marina's bonny smile and the golden fields each side? Why is my house shaken to bits but not I myself? Why has Marina come?

Jim woke from his second delusion. Marina Lampard had come not for a fight or a kiss, nor indeed for anything to do with herself, which now seemed to her a poor thing. Her dress was not sexual modesty but mourning, as much mourning as if she had come to Jim in black bombazine. Jim saw, in an access of weariness, that he must pick up the weapons he had set down, and set off again, his target over his shoulder. Yet that he could do, a hundred times, if necessary, for it was as nothing to what Marina had before her. It was a matter just to wait until Marina said what she had come to say.

Mrs Lampard looked down.

She said: "Sophy has leukemia."

Jim's world, so carefully rebuilt on its new foundation of happiness, a second time disintegrated. Jim's heart overflowed with pity, not just for the girl and her mother, but for his lost illusion. He had believed that the circle of the haunted comprised just Jack and himself and John Walker, and never thought that it would pass into the world of women and children. Jim said: "She will not die, Marina. I will ensure she does not die."

She turned up a face full of rage. Jim saw that her grief and fury did not spare the man she loved. "She starts treatment on Friday. They've cut off all her hair!" Her hands shook with horror.

Jim took a second step towards her and checked himself. "She will not die."

Marina turned her face up to him again. Jim saw that there was, after all, red at the lips and a little black in the eyes. Her scent made him swoon.

"She will not die."

They were drifting away again and so he started speaking: "Sophy will not die. Certain heroes succeeded in returning to the light, among them Theseus and Orpheus. Heracles wounded Hades himself. Also courageous and faithful women, Alcestis

210

and Persephone, the consort of Hades, who returned with her mother, Demeter, for half of each year . . ."

Marina said: "I'll exchange my life for my daughter's. You must tell me what I must do. I'm not frightened of dying."

It's not just dying you have to fear, my darling, when you pass through the Gate of Air.

"No," said Jim.

"Yes," said Marina.

"Marina, I will bring Sophy back. Then maybe you'll forgive me."

"I forgive you."

"You have people who depend on you in this world. I have nobody, unless you count Argos." He turned back to the house, where the dog was at the sit, watching them without concentration, as if he understood they had business and did not wish to intrude. "Anyway, I might fail and then you really will have no choice. I shall go down to Hell and bring Sophy back, but on one condition and it is this, and it is very hard for you."

Marina looked as if she could not imagine anything harder than what was now passing between them.

"Marina, you must tell me why Jeanie wants your husband among the dead."

She shuddered, as if the mention of the name might materialise the named.

"I don't know," she said.

"Yes, you do."

"I don't know, believe me, Jim."

Jim turned away. He did not, after all, have the heart to force her. Even if he had not liked her, he would not have forced her. He would never again force anybody, woman or man, to act against inclination. For Marina to answer, she must also answer why her marriage to Lampard had been a catastrophe, why she had borne just a single child, why she was so unhappy that she wished she were dead.

Jim, he is my husband. He may not like me any more, but he is still my husband.

I know.

"I . . ."

She stopped. Jim would never know what she wanted to say. She smiled from under her eyelids.

I'm a bad wife and a bad mother, Jim. I could only have improved.

Marina raised her head again. "Will you let me pray for you?"

"Who on earth to?"

You promised to stop being such a prick.

Did I?

You did.

Jim thought: We'd have gotten along together pretty well. Jim sensed a softening or abrasion of his nature that he imagined must occur when a man and woman choose each other and accept the consequences. He felt his soul, with its stone limbs and gaping Cycladic stare, like a toy in her dainty fingers. She reached out and plucked at the button of his coat. Then she climbed into her car.

212

Jim said: "Thank you for Jack's flowers, Marina. Nothing could have been more beautiful and kind."

You wouldn't even let me say goodbye to my only friend!

You said you'd forgiven me.

Forgiven, not forgotten.

They were falling again into reverie. Jim, in his mind's eye, was holding her around her waist, tending her broken heart. He thought: She'll change her mind. I must give her something to do.

He said: "With your permission, Marina, I'll also call Husham Tarabulsi in Paris. He saved my life in Baghdad in the war and he will save Sophy."

She said nothing. She was unable to leave. Jim thought: I will have to turn and leave.

"Jim! Wait!"

When I first saw you, coming through the door of my husband's house, I thought you were a like a god. My heart began to shake. I could not speak. My tongue would not do what it was told. There was ringing in my ears. I was cold all over. I could not see. I thought that if . . . Oh forget it!

From beneath the rim of her sunglasses, a round tear rolled down, rested for a moment on the ridge of her cheekbone, then splashed down in her lap. The electric window closed. She reached up to lock the door, and there, where her hand rested a moment against the glass, Jim placed his own against it.

He watched her drive away, the horsebox swinging and bumping behind her. He ran inside, up to his room, then to the attic and up the ladder and onto the roof. When he could no longer see the cavalcade, he whispered: I cannot love you as I would like and, as I believe, you would like. I can only fight for you. He came down to find Argos amid the glass on the nursery landing. He said: "Since when were you permitted upstairs, sir? Do I intrude on your kennel? I do not, and therefore you do not come to my bedrooms." Then he relented. "We can't wait, lad. We can't wait for harvest. Otherwise the child will die. We have to invite Jeanie here now."

Outside, he spat on his finger and held it up to the wind. The wind was coming from the west, blowing away from the house, and strong enough to rattle the leaves in the oaks. It was a good, warm, drying wind. From the stable, he brought a can of petrol, and the stub end of one of John's roll-up cigarettes, then thought better of the last — shame on you, Jim Smith! — and went into the house and found some book matches from a footballers' restaurant he'd once been to on the A101 near Chipstable. He felt as if he were walking a narrow ledge and below him lay his inconsolable yearning for Marina. He concentrated on the most routine of farm tasks. He brought the cow and calf into the stable and folded the ewes in the paddock nearest the house. In these tasks, Argos bustled ahead of him, pleased with his purpose. At sundown, Jim shut him in his kennel.

He said: "I have to burn the crop. It is too dangerous for you. I'll have to shut you in."

For a while, he stood in the dark kitchen by the telephone. He did that because he was certain Marina was doing the same and also that she was too proud and tough to call him. He said to himself that she knew he loved her, and that heart spoke to heart over the ten miles between their houses without need of telephones, but his mind fell into a despair. He imagined her standing in her nightgown in darkness. The thought of Marina in her nightgown caused him to swoon. He thought: Marina, I would have you hold your breath and let it out in pure happiness. Perhaps if he called and hung up, even before she could drop her hand to the receiver, then she would know who it was that had called and why and would be comforted.

The sound of the telephone made him jump.

Jim, please answer. I've changed my mind. I can't let you do it.

Pick up the phone, Jim Smith, or you can kiss goodbye to any hope of getting inside my . . .

Jim, please.

He lifted the receiver, as it were idly or experimentally, and heard a booming voice.

"Who is it, please?"

"IT'S GLORIANA."

"Ah, Mrs Gainer, what a surprise!"

"Well, I thought I should jolly well give you a call. To thank you for what you did. I knew all along you were a good chap, whatever anybody else said."

Jim was at a loss. "What have I done, Glory?"

"Don't be modest!"

It is certain that nobody up to then had ever accused Jim of being modest.

"Come on! I'm told that dreadful Richard Dark is baying for your guts."

"Well, Glory, he may be, but what is it I have done?"

"Go on with you! Eileen Medley told me that you paid the village's lawyers' bill."

"Glory, I must not claim credit for something that I have not done. I sent Mrs Medley a hundred pounds towards the Commons Committee's legal costs."

"Don't be so ridiculous. Nobody could be so stingy! I don't believe you. And nor does Richard Dark, so I'd watch your back, Jim Smith. Anyway, to business. Are you coming out with hounds on Thursday? I can mount you."

Jim felt a temporary alarm. Then he said, with more good manners than truthfulness, "It would be an honour and a pleasure."

After Mrs Gainer hung up, Jim stood for a while. For the first time, he wondered if perhaps his life should not be prolonged beyond necessity. Then he ran upstairs, and on to the roof, looked out to the floodlit pepper-pot tower of Mount Royal House. For a moment, he wondered what Marina saw in him, but did not proceed. Should he go to the seaside on a calm day, like Theocritus' shepherd, and see what his face looked like in the water? There was, he decided, no accounting for taste, least of all among women, and particularly not among women who pay their husbands' adversaries' legal bills. Jim whispered: Marina Lampard, it is impossible to exaggerate how much I admire you. You are everything I am not. What on earth do you see in me?

Outside, the moon was not yet risen. In the darkness, Jim could feel the wind gusting. He thought: Of course, last night's lightning. A fire could have been smouldering in the wet corn all day till the wind got hold of it. His courage returned to him. His reveries of Marina he set to the side. He crawled into the wheat and found the tramline where the tractor driver who had drilled the field had turned from the headland, and the wind had dried the stalks to the root. Marina, Marina, Marina. He uncapped the tank, filled the cap with petrol, bunched four stalks and dribbled them with liquid. The match took at once, climbed up the stalks and then the wind caught the flame, began to play with it, bent it double so it caught on the downwind stalks. Jim crawled back the way he had come.

He turned and saw the fire had caught. He began to fear he might not get away. Turning round, he smacked into Argos.

"What are you doing here, dog? How did you get out of your kennel?"

Argos sniffed at the ground. Jim saw the lie of the corn was not natural. The stalks had been uprooted and laid cross-ways, as if to cover something. He reached out to clear the stalks away, and leaped backwards. Argos howled. Before them the two jaws of the man-trap had closed on a stook of wheat.

"Are you all right, dog? For God's sake, lad."

Jim ran his hands down the dog's flanks to his haunches and then his feet. Argos was all right. He grabbed the trap by its jaws, but it would not budge.

Smoke and smuts were filling his eyes. All a-fumble, Jim found the stake and weight that held the trap in place, uprooted them, and dragged the whole thing after him. All the while, he cursed John Walker. Jim thought: John has his own plans to deal with the supernatural, the stupid idiot.

How many times, dog, will you save my life?

Back at the house, he returned the petrol tank and the trap to the stable, burned in the kitchen sink the only match he had used, and stood by the stove. After a while he rose, went to the broken window and listened. There was a tumbling roar as of moving heavy furniture. Through the trees he could see a lick of flame like a solar corona. Jim called 999 and asked for the fire brigade. The first of the fire engines found him thirteen minutes later at the gate, stained with smoke, chaff in his hair, tears in his eyes, wringing his hands.

Gordon McCain came up in his Land Rover, which didn't surprise Jim. What surprised him was the man's face. McCain said: "Must have been them hippies. I seen them snooping around here."

"The guys that work for you, Gordon?"

The police officer lifted his head. Serves you right, McCain, Jim said under his breath, for entertaining greedy thoughts.

CHAPTER
FIFTEEN

Argos

The summer was in decline. Jim lost his capacity for action. One day he received a letter. The stamp was French and the postmark Paris. Inside was a Valentine's card, which was strange, since it was not February. On the front, printed, was the phrase: "To my only Valentine". Inside was a drawing in ballpoint pen of a heart, pierced by an arrow, and inky droplets of blood.

Sometimes he stood in Marina's garden, which he now saw, as if for the first time, because it was hers. Mist hung like gauze on the box hedges and hid the boles of the cypresses. On the stone pavement, Jim felt enclosed. He felt that Marina had made the garden not for herself, or for spiteful women to criticize one day a year, or for some metropolitan magazine to spread across a double page, but for some companion she wished to please in her imagination. He felt he might stand in some spot where she had stood or knelt.

Jim understood that Marina had made Paradise Farm as a scolded child makes a house in long grass, where she could live in her imagination, with just Sophy, or perhaps with Sophy and a decent man. Without in any way having planned such a thing, Jim unpicked the convolvulus from the box and cleared the weeds from the roots. He guyed the cypresses where their tips had bent in the wind, clipped the box and swept leaves fine as tea fannings off the pavement. He brought up sand and relaid the stones where they were unsteady. On the bark of a young beech, he carved Marina's name and wondered, daft fellow that he was, that somebody coming by in a hundred years would see letters four inches tall and think that some poor man must have liked this Marina person.

He attended the auction at Brightwell, bought unsteady furniture and peeling pictures. In organising Jack's affairs at the Bothy, he found, in no time at all, in an old Dutch document cabinet, Mavis Bolingbroke's deed of assignment for Haze Common.

From an architectural salvage yard in Chipstable, Jim bought a stack of eighteenth-century window glass and a rotary cutter from the ironmonger across the road. In late afternoon, as he glazed his bedroom, seeing the light fall on the carpet, Jim thought: This room has become dear to me. This, and the landing full of light, and the stair-rods and bannisters vanishing from sight, and the Toledo chest with its studs and decayed velvet, and the bath worn to the zinc by hot water, and the howl of wind under the front door, and the lilac branches scratching at the panes, and the rustle of dried rose petals in the Qianlong dish at the end of the long corridor, and the light broken into colours by the cut-glass door handles and the deep hanging-cupboard with the scent of Marina's summer dresses. These sensations of light and wind and warmth are my portion of happiness that comes to me, like a contested inheritance, twenty years on and all the more welcome for that. Jim's heart stuttered with a premonition of winter at Paradise Farm, of silence and white light engulfing the long rooms and, at the end, tottering on bare feet in the gusts of light, a child who was and who would be more fortunate than her parents. He saw that happiness had something to do with dying, with the ability to die. Happiness was the counterpart, not of sorrow, but of death. Then, one morning when the mist still lay heavy on the garden, Jim Smith straightened and looked up.

He did not look at the black stubble. He saw in his imagination a dog racing in a great circle round the field, as if after a raised hare.

Argos let out such a howl that Jim jumped.

"Don't you dare make that sound! Get in the house!"

Argos was on his haunches, his fur bristling the length of his backbone, glaring at Jim in a way he had never done before. Jim could see that he was in an equilibrium, torn between obedience and terror. Anything could happen. Jim spoke gently: "You cannot come with me, do you understand? Wait here for me."

He opened the back door and Argos slunk in.

As he turned, Jim thought: I could just ignore it, come out in an hour, see if it was still here. Then he raised his head, and saw the saluki speeding along the hedge. It passed out of view. *Sunt aliquid manes.* There's such a thing as ghosts.

Jim stopped. He did not think he had the strength to walk. He felt he had passed out of his own world and was walking on water or air. He felt a compulsion to fall and, in falling, lose everything and with it the fear of falling. In his mind, thoughts flitted like little birds. Why interfere in the business of the supernatural? Why not let the dying die? Poor Sophy is so hurt, how can she be put together again? Marina is young and will have other children. Let the dying die and the living go on in the green earth and blue air, while cities rise and are destroyed about them. And he, Jim, would be gone and Marina would know that he had failed, not why he had failed.

In the gap in the hedge, the saluki passed again. Jim shook his head. If the world were just a matter of knowledge, he would have been well fitted to be Marina's champion. He had come, by the force of his concentration, to a state of knowledge reached by perhaps only one or two persons in a generation, and yet that was not enough. It was necessary to act. Jim had not the courage to act.

But something in him had been altered beyond restitution. His self was more than his knowledge. His love for Marina, blocked from its proper channel, had overflowed into unfrequented parts of his nature, and one of those was his courage. He saw, with an insight that would have been far beyond him just a week before, why Marina loved him. She loved him because she believed, in the depths of her heart, that Jim alone of all men would give his life for her. His mortality was his ally. Jim understood at last that Marina had seen the apparition that night of the dinner party at Mount Royal House. She had also seen that Jim and not her faithless husband had stood up to protect her child.

Jim began to run, pulling at the gun in his side-holster. It was that bitch's doing and now she would pay the price. Diomede struck her on the wrist when she tried to interfere in the fight at Troy and he cut her tendon so she had to go crying to her father. And I will put a bullet in her pretty face to teach her not to meddle again in the affairs of men.

Jim passed into the black stubble. The stench of ash and wet smoke caused him to choke. It was the smell he remembered that day as he lay in Bab al-Hawa with the blood pouring from his wound, thinking he would die not of his wound but of cold and that his chattering teeth would shake him to pieces. In the fog, he lost all sense of direction. He cried: "What do you want?"

His words were engulfed in the mist.

He spun round and shouted again: "Jeanie, what do you want?"

In the mist, he did not know where he was facing. He did not know his left from his right, or his up from his down. He bent on one knee and put his hand on the stubble.

What do you want, Goddess?

τί θέλεις, Θεά;

σέ θέλω, τέκνον.

I want *you*, child.

Jim felt as if he had been struck in the head. As the blow reverberated, he saw for a moment through the veils of his stupidity. It was not that she wanted revenge on Lampard. Lampard was a matter of indifference to her. Had she not told him so when she came to him in the dream? She had cursed Marina not because she was Lampard's wife, but because she was Jim's darling. How could he hope to conceal his passions from an Immortal! She had seen, that evening at Mount Royal House, what he and Marina had not seen and only just begun to feel one for the other; and that is why she came into the room and struck little Sophy with her distaff, murderous jealous slut that she is. That is why she dried up the cattle and drove off the bees and killed the lambs and at last, when Jim saw Marina in the lighted window, smashed every window in his house.

In a horror of foreboding, Jim turned. Standing at the corner of the field, the black stubble to his flanks, was Argos. Along the top of his head, and down his back, were streaks of blood. Jim thought Argos had been whipped and then he realised the dog must have jumped through one of the broken windows. Jim thought: How could I be so foolish as to forget about the windows? It is the mistake of my life that will never be pardoned or made good. He turned and cried: "You bitch!"

Jim turned again. Argos took a step forward. He was swaying as if in a high wind. Jim saw that he wanted to come to his friend, but he was just too frightened and his heart was breaking. Jim was running. The sharp stubble pricked the soles of his feet through his boots. Argos was still on his feet, but he was like a stool or table, maintained just by his geometry. Jim seemed to come no closer.

"No!" cried Jim.

Argos leaned to his left, then toppled over. Jim thought it would be all right if he could catch his dog's last breath and look once more into his soft eyes. When he arrived, Argos was warm, but his eyes were blank and there was no breath from his mouth and no heartbeat. Jim turned back. There was nothing to be seen in the fog. His pistol fizzed in the fog, again and again and again, till the magazine was empty. Jim stood in the stink of wet earth and burnt cartridge powder. He bent down and hoisted the dog onto his neck and walked, head bowed under the weight, back to the house.

Jim buried Argos beside the fence. He knew that the hole must be large and deep, and it would tire him, and so he worked away, grim-faced. He did not want his dog to be cramped in the hole. Looking at the body stretched out on the leaves, he said: "Wait for me on the other bank, lad. I shan't be long."

Then, recognising that there was nobody to see him and that this was a matter between him and Argos, and only Argos and him, for the first time in his adult life, and for what would certainly be the last, Jim cried. He cried for Argos, and for Jack and for Marina, and for his dead parents, for the infirmity of mortals and the plain damn wickedness of the gods. The force of his grief carried him on, as he laid the body side on into the hole, bent the head between the forepaws, and replaced the earth.

He straightened, painfully. John Walker was standing in front of him, dead drunk, shotgun at the shoulder.

"You bastard. You killed my damn dog."

"That's enough, John."

"I knew you . . ."

"I said: That's enough, John. Even if you shoot, you cannot injure me. I'll send on what I owe you. And a gift. Jack left you the cottage. You're free now, I promise, to live and to die."

Jim walked towards the house. John raised the twenty-bore and clicked off the safety catch. Then, evidently because John could not shoot a man in the back, Jim felt him lower the weapon. Jim understood that he had at last achieved his goal and had no attachment to anybody or anything under the sun. He might have been dead. He said to himself: The trouble with you, Jim Smith, is that no way can you retain motivated staff.

CHAPTER
SIXTEEN

The Gate of Air

If Jim had any regrets, they were all for the present. He would stop to watch the oak leaves come spiralling down in the still air or smell the coal fires from the village council houses at sundown or hear the mistle-thrushes chattering in the holly. He wrote a will, leaving his property to Marina Lampard, but for a pension for John Walker and *Venus in a Groovy Hat*. The picture he sold to the Duke of Essex to hang in the billiard room of his new country estate, Mount Royal House.

Jim took the train to Paris. At the *Centre Médical* in Clichy, he found Dr Tarabulsi in a herd of men and women, the smallest of whom must have been twice his height. Jim called out to the back of his scrubs: *A moment, please, master.*

Husham Tarabulsi stopped and with him his companions. He said in English: "Excuse me, ladies and gentlemen, one of my countrymen is here." He gestured to them to be patient, turned and faced Jim with a look of unbending resolution.

Heavens, thought Jim, he thinks I'm going to kill him! He can see I carry a gun! He thinks I'm an assassin! Of course, he's the most famous Iraqi Arab alive and must have scores of enemies. Jim lifted his arms from his side to show he would not use the gun and smiled.

Is it your judgement that Miss Sophy is now truly out of danger?

Dr Tarabulsi was not inclined to carry on a private conversation in inaccurate Arabic. He answered in English: "Are you her father?"

There isn't a father in the case, master.

Dr Tarabulsi said: "It had nothing at all to do with me. The progress in the case is due, first, to the indomitable courage of the young patient, second, to the devoted care of her mother, and third, to the limitless mercy of God. I repeat: I did nothing."

Well, thought Jim, that should exhaust the etiology. Yet he suspected that Dr Tarabulsi was not content in his diagnosis, not by a long distance. There was something that troubled him about Mlle Sophy's recovery, and he was continuing to carry out tests. Jim was wise enough to see that that was the only reason why Dr Tarabulsi gave him the time of day. He felt on him the force of Dr Tarabulsi's intellect, which was by far the most powerful he had ever encountered. Yet that mind, however powerful, was a mere instrument in the service of the doctor's humanity. Jim thought: Here is the goal of all philosophy, the Perfect Man!

"And how is your recovery, dear friend?"

Never forgets a patient, either.

Thanks be to God, master.

"I am happy that have you done something with the life that God gave back to you."

I intend, master, to follow the road wherever it leads.

"Well, don't leave it too long, dear friend. You'll find the ladies in room 1896."

Through the porthole in the door, Jim saw that Marina was asleep, curled up in her chair, her little stockinged feet pulled up beneath her bottom. Sophy, too, was asleep, breathing oxygen. They seemed both to have travelled back in time, breathing pure air, to the place where they had been happy, free of all standing and possessions, sisters and friends. Jim learned at last that to be mortal, but also to live, was all there was, and he must reach out and grasp the moment and press it to his lips.

He flattered himself that they would not forget him, and that they would find his remains on Brightwell Links, and raise a mound for him and put a cairn on top to guide the weekend sailors racing before the wind into Brightwell harbour. He saw that a vagueness of manner, only just now evident, becomes Marina's salient characteristic, to the great exasperation of her daughter and grandsons: that, and her obstinacy. Marina, you could have had any man in the world, why didn't you marry again? For an instant, Jim saw her in extreme old age, dozing in the sunshine under the windows of Paradise Farm before half a crust spread with honey. Through the tall window of the drawing room, a housemaid named Eufimia Polinova looks down at her mistress.

Enough of all that!

Jim did not open the door.

It is for mortals to accept their fate, and to take what has been spared them from the gods. As he walked away down the hospital corridor, Jim thought: Am I so very unfortunate? It is not given to every man to love a mortal woman. Outside, in the hospital carpark, the swallows were twittering on the telephone lines, half-flown to sunshine.

And each morning as dawn flecks the sky with red, he rises from the lovely goddess' bed to hunt all day on steep Taygetus or in the cool groves of Tempe, with fleet-footed Argos leading the chiming pack, in a world without end.

Also available in ISIS Large Print:

The Great Lover

Jill Dawson

Nell Golightly is living out her widowhood in Cambridgeshire when she receives a strange request. A Tahitian woman, claiming to be the daughter of the poet Rupert Brooke, writes to ask what he was like. How did he sound, what did he smell like, how did it feel to wrap your arms around him? So Nell turns her mind to 1909 when, as a seventeen-year-old housemaid, she first encountered the young poet. He was already causing a stir — not only with his poems and famed good looks, but also by his taboo-breaking behaviour and radical politics. Intrigued, she watched as Rupert skilfully managed his male and female admirers, all of whom seemed to be in love with him. Soon Nell realised that despite her good sense, she was falling for him too. But could he love a housemaid? Was he, in fact, capable of love at all?

ISBN 978-0-7531-8340-3 (hb)
ISBN 978-0-7531-8341-0 (pb)

The Parish of Hilby

Mary E. Mann

When Mr James Massey moves to the Parish of Hilby and becomes the new tenant of Wood Farm he is soon the centre of attention.

Invited to events within the typical small Norfolk Village by the local residents, Massey finds himself attending village concerts, a garden party, high tea at the Grange and even dinner at the Vicarage.

As the residents warm to him so too do the hearts of two women, Helen Smythe and Pollie Freeman. When Pollie mistakes his affections for a proposal James realises it is Helen he favours above all. But Pollie has informed her parents of the engagement and in a small village where word travels quickly will James have a choice?

Few punches are pulled in portraying the rigid class system of the time, from the squire to the vicar, the tenant farmer to the most impoverished labourer.

ISBN 978-0-7531-8234-5 (hb)
ISBN 978-0-7531-8235-2 (pb)

Playing with the Moon

Eliza Graham

Selected for the World Book Day Spread the Word promotion

Shattered by a recent bereavement, Minna and her husband Tom retreat to an isolated village on the Dorset coast. Walking on the beach one day, they unearth a human skeleton. The remains are soon identified as those of a black American GI who, it seems, drowned during a wartime exercise 60 years before.

Growing increasingly preoccupied with the dead soldier's fate, Minna befriends a melancholy elderly woman, Felix, who lived in the village during the war. As Minna coaxes Felix's story from her, it becomes clear that the old woman knows more about the dead GI than she initially let on. Felix's final shocking confession allows her to come to terms with an event that has cast a shadow over her life, and helps Minna to begin to accept her own loss.

ISBN 978-0-7531-8170-6 (hb)
ISBN 978-0-7531-8171-3 (pb)

Then We Came to the End

Joshua Ferris

"How we hated our coffee mugs! Our mouse pads, our desk clocks, our daily calendars, all the contents of our desk drawers. Even the photos of our loved ones taped to our computer monitors for uplift and support turned to cloying reminders of time served . . ."

Then We Came to the End is about how we spend our days and too many of our nights. It is about being away from friends and family, about sharing a stretch of stained carpet with a group of strangers we call colleagues. It is about sitting all morning next to someone you deliberately cross the road to avoid at lunchtime.

Joshua Ferris's fabulous novel is the story of your life, and mine. It is the story of our times.

ISBN 978-0-7531-8224-6 (hb)
ISBN 978-0-7531-8225-3 (pb)

Please return by the last date shown
Flintshire Library and Information Service
Dychweler erbyn y dyddiad olaf uchod
Gwasanaeth Llyfrgell a Gwybodaeth Sir y Fflint